The Deadbeat Club

John Lugo-Trebble

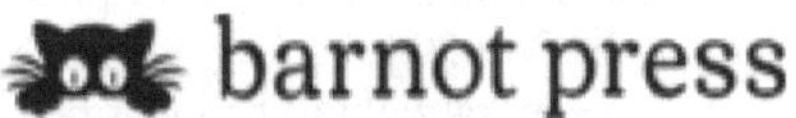 barnot press

2020 edition published by barnot press.
Copyright © 2020 John Lugo-Trebble
John Lugo-Trebble asserts his moral right to be identified as the author of the
work. All rights reserved. No part of this publication can be produced in any form
or by any means without the prior permission of the author.
Cover Design by John Lugo-Trebble
Author Photo by David Lugo-Trebble
Typeset by David Lugo-Trebble
Contact: john@johnlugotrebble.net
ISBN:
978-1-9160596-1-0

DEDICATION

To My Husband David:
Everywhere

To Nadine:
You looked after us all. We miss you.

ACKNOWLEDGMENTS

I would like to thank my husband David Lugo-Trebble whose support in writing this series has been invaluable. He challenges me to not only be a better writer but a better person with each passing day.

I would like to thank my sister Kasandra Showers and my brother Jose Ayala as well as all my wonderful nephews and nieces who continue to give me hope for the next generation.

I would also like to thank Alys Lugo-Trebble, Rosie Lugo-Trebble, Tilly Lugo-Trebble, Cass Simpson, Gabriela Oravetz, Andrew Hawthorne, Robert Blasi, Natascha de los Angeles Fusari-Pratt, Josh Carr, Michael Belsky, Alvin Fung, Austin Pratt, Kristen Galvin, Renay Schlereth, Heather Privrat, Eilidh Armstrong, Barbara Armstrong, Brigitte Ariel, Tyler Dempster, Georgiana Steele Nelsen, Jennifer Kircher Carr, Clay Adams, Jolene McIlwain, Pamela Bailie, Henry Padron, Seana Graham, Bethan Grimshaw, Jen Alexander, Jenny Cole, Daniela Norris, Story Talk, Hipocampo Children's Books, The Metta Centre and New York City. Your support is one of the greatest gifts a friend and writer could ever ask for.

AUTHORS NOTE

Characters in this book from time to time use a mixture of English and Spanish, commonly known as "Spanglish." Readers should be able to enjoy the dialogue with little difficulty or previous knowledge of Spanish.

As the book is set in 1993, please be aware that LGBTQ+ language and terminology is reflective of the time and not meant to cause any purposeful offence.

There are many references to music throughout the novel. The use of music is strictly for narrative purposes and should not be seen as an endorsement, affiliation or collaboration of any sort.

Part One

One

Cuchi had insisted we wear wigs for Wigstock.

"Ya bitches are NOT going to embarrass me on one of the holiest of drag days." She said to us.

James had on a blonde wig with a pony tail held up by a headband like Grace Jones in *Boomerang*. Si had on a long wavy frizzy wig that was inspired by the album cover to Belinda Carlisle's *Runaway Horses*. I went for the bob look she had in the video for "Runaway Horses." It was one of *our* songs. That's right, we had songs now. We had just had our three monthaversary (Si's word) and though Labor Day meant that the summer was pretty much over, at that moment it felt like summer could go on forever. The sun was shining. It was hot but not too humid. Mother Nature herself was making sure that we all had a good time.

Tompkins Square Park was overflowing with all sorts of people from old and young, gay to straight and everything in between. Everyone was there celebrating wigs, heels and all things drag. There were scenes of love and unity set to the music of Deee-Lite, Deborah Harry and RuPaul.

Performers I had never heard of before the summer now felt like friends even though I hadn't meant them: Mistress Formika, Tabboo!, Flotilla DeBarge and Lady Bunny carried us through the day when they usually led us to sunrise at the clubs. My head was spinning with all the music and laughs. I felt so high, like I could touch the tip of the Empire State Building with my hands.

Si had his arms around me and we were moving along to "House of Love" as RuPaul got us all dancing. Cuchi was in her element dancing next to James who had his arms in the air. Cuchi was dressed in a similar style to Tina Turner when she performed "Proud Mary" in that fringe skirt. She too had a headband on but her wig was pushed back like La Lupe. My mother had introduced Cuchi to La Lupe, who had been my Uncle Jose's favorite singer. She was now Cuchi's latest obsession. Not content with just meeting Si, my mother had sort of become everyone's mom in the group and sometimes I thought they enjoyed her company more than mine. I was lucky though, how many kids had a mom who accepted them being gay? How many had a mother who accepted them being gay and having a boyfriend? How many had a mother who traded clothes with their gay son's drag queen best friend? Truth is I was beyond lucky.

I sunk back into Si's arms. His wig draped over mine and the reddish strands tickled my nose. I looked up at him. He looked back into my eyes and gave me a peck on the lips. My beeper interrupted the moment going any further. After having stayed out all night, my mother decided she wasn't going through that hell again so she bought me a beeper.

"Your mom?" Si said.

Without needing to look at it, I knew it was her. I pulled it out and there was just the number "2." That had become her code to not stay out late because of *that* night. I didn't get home till 2pm the following day.

"Guess that means you have to go home tonight?"

I turned around and looked at Si who looked down at me with a hint of sadness. I felt that knot in my stomach I got when I knew we had to be apart. RuPaul was shouting about love. I didn't want to think about spending the night apart.

"I can always ask?"

Si smiled and kissed me again on the lips. Our wigs together must have looked a big mess. He grabbed my hand and said, "Let's go find a phone."

We told James and Cuchi that I needed to find a phone. Cuchi shouted out "tell Maria I love huh."

As he was taller, Si led us through the crowds of wigs, headpieces, glitter, pot smoke and smiles. We bumped in to Tisha and Wanda who were dressed as nuns in miniskirts with shiny red thigh high boots.

"Hey Baby!" Tisha said as she bent down and gave us kisses."Them trash finally leave you alone?"

"For now." I hadn't thought about Anthony or Melanie *fucking* Sputano all summer long. I hadn't thought about school or how I had come out to everyone just before school let out. Thanks to the asbestos found in public schools, I didn't have to think about any of that for at least another week.

"Well anymore trouble, you let us know." Wanda said.

"I will." They were better protection than any cops in the city. I doubt the cops would have done anything to Anthony that night near the piers. "Cuchi and James are in the middle over there." I pointed in the direction we had come.

"Thanks baby." They responded in unison.

We found a phone booth just outside the park but there was someone dressed as Carmen Miranda using it, so we waited. I wrapped my arms around Si's slim waist and put my head against his chest. I could feel his heartbeat as he kissed me on the head.

"You okay?"

"Just enjoying the moment."

Carmen winked at us when she was done. I loved being downtown. Anything was possible downtown. Anything was possible away from The Bronx. I took a deep breath and looked at Si. He had a face like he was waiting to be told if his answer was right or wrong on *Jeopardy*.

"Hi Mami."

"*Mijo*. Everything ok?"

"*Sí* Ma. Yea."

"You enjoying the festival?"

"Yea Ma, listen." I took a deep breath and my voice became more child like. "Can I stay at Si's tonight?"

Silence.

"Ma?"

"*Sí*, fine. I want you home early tomorrow. Ok. *¿Me entiendes?*

"Yea. I understand. Thank you."

I smiled at Si and he walked over and wrapped his arms around my waist. He kissed me on neck.

"Thank you Mrs. Morales." He said into the phone loud.

"*De nada* Simon." She said. "Have fun and remember that things are going to be different when school starts again."

"Love you Mami!"

"Dios de bendigan, mijos."

She had been pretty flexible over the summer with me staying at Si's, hanging out and having a summer job. It was the main reason that I knew most of those names on the stage. We partied and had as much fun as we could. With the summer coming to an end, I knew that would change.

Si's parents had agreed to let him move into his own place in the Village for his second year. I wasn't sure how cool my mother would be about letting me stay there. It didn't matter that night though. I grabbed his hand and we headed back to find Cuchi and James. I no longer felt like Cinderella at the ball.

"Ey Papi. She letting you hang out?" James asked.

I nodded and smiled.

Cuchi wrapped her arms around me. "I love huh."

"Oh she said not to lose her headband."

"I bet those are words you never thought you would say." Cuchi responded. She then pulled out a blunt from her small glittery purse which I was sure she had also borrowed from my mother.

James gave Cuchi a disapproving look. "Mmhmm. Always one. You can take the girl out of the ghetto."

Cuchi arched her eyebrows. "Oh you don't want any?"

"Why so violent?" James said.

I laughed with them. They were a double act and I was finally in on the joke. I did sometimes wonder what kind of couple they would have made, had they not been like sisters.

Si snatched the blunt from Cuchi's hand. "Well if you won't light it."

"*Ay desgraciado.*"

He blew her a kiss and lit the blunt. It was a good thing the park already smelled of pot. After passing it between us, it made its way to the group standing next to us. There was a couple I couldn't help but notice. One was a muscle boy and the guy he had his arms around was slimmer, effeminate and dressed in a blue velvet pant suit with neon green sunglasses. At first glance, they looked a bit odd together but then a few months ago, I would have said the same about Si and myself. Thing is, they looked happy. James always talked about energy, that when the energy was right, it didn't matter what it looked like to other people. I smiled at them as I put my arms around Si.

We danced all the way till after Donna Giles' performance of "Give Me Luv" which James insisted we stay for. The square had gone from drag show to outdoor club and we threw our hands in the air as Donna sang her heart into the microphone.

After she finished, we headed back to the West Village for some food at Tiffany's. As we walked crosstown, any time we got a look from people on the street, Cuchi would smile and yell out "Its natural" just as nasal as Tabboo! had sung that afternoon. It was infectious as was the performance; and by the time we crossed 7th Avenue S, we had all said it at least once.

Tiffany's was busy when we got there. We weren't the only ones who had come from Wigstock and in that moment the place looked like an unofficial after party. I had come to look at the West Village as home so I knew very little about the East Village or that part of town. Si and I had explored a little during the summer when we were looking for places to be alone without any interruption. That day though East and West didn't matter as much as wigs and make up, at least at Tiffany's it didn't.

Billy sat us towards the back of the diner and Cuchi couldn't help herself.

"Stop looking at my ass. Ain't never gonna happen."

"No scenes." He said. It had become a running joke and given that more than half the customers were in some form of drag, we all smiled.

"Oh Billy look around." James said as he tapped him on the right cheek. "It's like a drag queen's purse exploded up in here." He then turned to Cuchi and took his wig off. "Gurl, I don't know how you wear these all the time. My head needs to breathe."

"I don't buy cheap wigs."

I saw Billy crack a smile as he put the menus down on the table and walked away.

As fun as the day had been, I agreed with James and took my wig off. Si followed. Cuchi looked at us all with the type of smile a proud mother would give.

"Well thank you for joining me today."

"Anytime." I said.

That was the truth. I would do anything for her or for anyone at the table. They were my family.

"So Si, when is the first house party?" James asked.

Si froze on the spot and if it were possible for him to go anymore white, he did at that moment. He was saved by Irena who had come to take our order. After she left, Cuchi persisted.

"Well, when? I need notice cos you know this look don't just happen."

"And yet at times, you would think she woke up like that."

"*¡Cabron!*" She said to James.

Si took a deep breath and said, "Well, it was going to be a surprise but as you bitches are nosey as hell and you just put me on the spot." He looked at me. "I thought it could be your birthday next week."

"What about my mom?" *It sounded lamer out loud than in my head.*

Si looked at me as he did when I was, in his words, being "too cute." He put his arm around me. "Don't worry. I already cleared it with her. She wants to make *pernil*, rice and beans for the party."

"*¡Wepa!*" Cuchi clapped loud which made Billy glare at her. "That's what I'm talking about."

The food came. We ate and talked about the coming school year. We skirted around the college talk as if it were a sink hole we were afraid of falling into. It was senior year for James, Cuchi and me. Si was starting his second year at NYU. I hadn't wanted to think about where I would apply to college because when I did, I felt sick at the thought of being away from Si and my friends. We knew a change was coming but at that moment, all that mattered was *us* sat at Tiffany's amongst the rest of the misfits.

Cuchi wanted to head down to the piers but Si and I gave each other that look that couples did when they wanted to be alone. James picked up on it and gave us both hugs. I watched him and Cuchi disappear around the corner down Christopher Street.

Si bent down to tie his shoe after we said our goodbyes and they had turned the corner. When he got up, I went to walk in the direction of West 4th Street Subway but he stopped me and suggested a detour. We walked down West 4th Street heading away from 7th Avenue South. They were the streets I fell in love with a few months ago; tree lined, brick houses with stoops and little black wrought iron fences and gates. Although it felt at times that the city moved with the speed of light, time slowed down on these small blocks. I knew where he was leading me. We stopped in front of a red brick building and he pointed up to the top two windows with a fire escape.

"Just think." He said. "Soon we'll be home in less than 5 minutes."

I leant against him. *Home.* I liked the way it sounded. The summer had felt like I had had multiple homes. I had stuff at his. There was my bedroom at my mom's. I had even left things at Cuchi's when we had sleepovers. "Well, your home." I said.

Si stepped in front of me and took my hand. He had this hurt look. "Hey, my home is your home." He said as he played with my fingers.

"You mean that?"

"Of course I do baby. What's up?"

I looked at the floor. I was my turn to look a little hurt. "I hate that summer is over and things are changing."

He put his finger under my chin and guided me upwards so I was looking at him. "Think of it as moving forward."

Si knew what to say to make me smile. It was his gift. I kissed him and took his hand in mine. We walked towards 8th Avenue and hailed a taxi instead of taking the subway.

"When are your parents back?"

"Tomorrow afternoon."

In the back of the taxi, he held my hand as we sped Uptown. In a way, the only difference between how his parent's street looked and the one he was moving to was that the houses were bigger. They were both tree lined and time slowed down on them.

As soon as we entered the house, he pushed me against the closed door and started kissing me. Both of us were breathing fast and neither of us could contain the feeling taking over us. I pulled his t-shirt off and led him up the stairs. By the time we had gotten to the top, he had pulled mine off. We left a trail of clothing from the door to his bedroom. Our naked bodies became one as we gave into one another.

"I love you Si." I said in broken breathes.

"I love you too Lu."

I closed my eyes as he kissed my neck. There was no doubt in my mind that I was going to miss the summer.

Two

I woke up in Si's arms with his chin on my shoulder. Strands of his dirty blonde hair tickled my left ear. His hair had become lighter over the summer. I snuggled back into him and opened my eyes, taking in the glow of the sunlight around the borders of the thick curtains that separated us from the world. I could tell it would be another sunny day. It seemed like all the days had been sunny since we met.

"Mmmm. Morning." He kissed me on the neck which sent a shiver up and down my body and I squirmed against him which made him hold me tighter.

"Good Morning to you too." I said.

"Do you have to go to Jackie's today?" He asked.

"Nope. She's in Sag Harbor for the week." Jackie had given me the keys to her loft so when she was out of town, I could go in and get her things in order. Working for a neurotic borderline alcoholic lesbian photographer had added to the magic that was my first summer, out and proud. "Don't your classes start today?"

Si shook his head. "Tomorrow's my first class."

"Oh."

"Yea."

His parents would be home later which meant we had our last morning in their house alone. It was a bit like our first morning together but without the fear of facing an angry mother. I thought about how much I would miss the easy travel between his parent's and mine but the promise of our space and what we could do with it was exciting. In a few days, we would be able to roll out of bed and pop to Tiffany's or The Espresso Bar or Manatus. We would be able to walk home after partying at Limelight or The Tunnel. Si was right, change is just about moving forward.

I turned around to face him and though we both had morning breath, it didn't matter. I never got tired of feeling his lips against mine.

Our eyes locked and he arched his eyebrows.

Si got out of bed to use the bathroom about 9am and I laid there looking at the room. Most of his stuff was already boxed up and in the corner. There was a box with my name on it that made me smile. He hadn't taken the posters down yet but the room had been stripped of his personality. It was more like a room with a bed in it than *his* bedroom.

When he returned from the bathroom he was wearing a forest green bathrobe that looked soft and carrying a Bloomingdales bag in his hand. He had a huge smile on his face as he put the bag down next to me on the bed.

"What's this?"

"Think of it as housewarming gift."

I sat up and looked in the bag. Inside was a light grey bathrobe of the same material he was wearing. "I love it."

"I thought you would need it in our new place."

"*Our* place." It still sounded weird to me when I said it.

"Yes Lu, *Our* place. Try it on."

I stood up and he held it open for me so I could step into it. The material was plush and it felt like I was wrapped in a dream. I kissed him and then followed him downstairs to the kitchen.

"I'm gonna miss this place." I said as he turned the coffee maker on. Si was on one side of the counter and I was on the other. There was sunlight coming through the doors that led onto a small patio.

He took my hands in his and kissed them. "We have so many beautiful things ahead of us baby."

I didn't know how to respond to those things but I loved hearing them. I loved that when he said them, they didn't sound creepy or cheesy. He believed them which made me believe them. It was one of his special powers.

"You want some pancakes?" I asked.

"Now you're talking."

I got up and joined him on the other side of the counter. The smell of coffee was filling the kitchen and although it wasn't the Café Bustelo that my mother made, the freshly ground Kona that his parents bought from Zabar's had become *our* morning smell. Si turned the radio on and we made breakfast together as we sang along to Duran Duran's "Come Undone." As 80's fans, we both loved that they were back and it had become a favorite of ours. *We had favorites. We had songs.*

After breakfast, we showered together and as I looked at our naked bodies, I didn't feel that we looked strange together. Not like when we first met and I wondered why he would be with me. My body didn't look as boyish next to his. Si was more toned than me but we looked right together. Maybe it wasn't me but how I saw myself that had changed. I had become more comfortable in my own body over the summer.

We put off having to say goodbye as long as we could by watching some TV, laying and talking on his bed. I knew that it wasn't a good idea to push it too far with my mother. She had been more than generous and I had to figure out a way to keep spending weeknights with Si in the future.

He walked me to the subway as he had done since we had first met. The sun was shining as we walked around the outside of The Museum of Natural History. Though it was a Tuesday, it felt like it could have been a Sunday. The streets weren't busy with people walking although the traffic was flowing steady on Columbus Avenue. There was a slight chill in the air which was a reminder that summer was on its way out but that the sun wasn't ready to say goodbye yet.

"So this is our last walk like this." I said as we turned onto W 81st Street.

"Next time it'll be a walk to West 4th.

"Or 14th."

He giggled. "You going to help me unpack Thursday?"

"I'll be there after I stop into Jackie's in the morning."

"I can't wait." He said.

When we got to the subway entrance, Si looked around before

giving me a kiss on the lips.

I got on the C train with a familiar dread in the pit of my stomach as it took me further Uptown. I took out my Walkman and put my headphones on. When I pressed play, I expected to hear ABBA *Gold* which I had bought over the summer but instead was met with the opening to "Deeper and Deeper." I stopped it, opened the Walkman and saw the handwritten label on the cassette: *Moving Forward.*

I smiled. Si must've put it into my walkman at some point in the morning. I danced inside my head even though outside, I was just bopping my head.

When I put my key into the door, I was humming along to Belinda Carlisle's "We Want the Same Thing." I put my bag down outside my bedroom and walked into the kitchen to find my mother sitting at the table with a cup of coffee. She was reading *El Diario.* She looked up when she saw me and smiled. I took my headphones off and walked over her to give her a kiss. As much as I felt like I didn't fit in The Bronx, it was my home and seeing how happy she was to see me, reminded me of that.

She looked at her watch and then up at me. I knew I was earlier than she expected and I could see how happy that made her.

"Nice evening, *mijo?*"

"It was fun." She didn't need to know how much fun, right?

"You hungry?"

I shook my head and went to the fridge to see what we had to drink. There was some freshly squeezed *limonada* in the pitcher so I poured myself a glass. I sat down across from her at the table as she went back to reading the paper.

"Ma, you know how school is starting late this year right?"

"Mhmmm." She responded not looking up from the paper.

"Well, you know how Si is moving into his own place on Thursday."

"Mhmmm." She still did not look up.

"Well..."

She put the newspaper down and looked at me. "*Ay mijo*, spit it out already. *¿Qué me preguntas?*

I took a deep breath. "Okay, well can I stay the night with him?"

"Okay, but don't you forget about dinner Friday."

Dinner was the perfect way to put her mind at ease. It was the way to stop these awkward moments. *Why was it harder for me to ask if I could stay the night with my boyfriend than it was to tell her I had one?*

"Ma, why don't we have dinner in the Village. You could see his new place, so you know where it is. I can invite James and Cuchi."

She looked at me as if she was looking for the catch. "Okay."

I was about to argue about how she needed to trust me and that I was getting older and then I heard what she had said, *Okay?*

"*Sí*, sounds fun."

There was something too easy about what had just happened but as it worked in my favor, I wasn't about to question it.

"Thanks Ma."

"Love you *mijo*."

I got up from the table and left my mother to read her newspaper in peace. I grabbed my bag and opened my bedroom door. Like me, my bedroom had changed over the summer. In addition to posters from *Teen Beat*, I had put up posters and political images from Gay Men's Health Crisis, Pride and Act Up. On my desk was a picture of Cuchi, James, Si and Me at my first ever Pride. On my nightstand was a picture of me and Si taken over the summer on the piers. The sun was setting and he had his arms around me. They were mementos of how much fun the summer had been.

I lay down on my bed and looked over at the picture I had of my Mom, Dad and Uncle Jose holding me as a baby. I think it was after my christening because my dad was in a suit. Since he had died before I could remember much about him, I found myself being able to think of him any way I wanted. *Of course he would have accepted a gay son; mom would have made sure of it.*

I put my headphones on and pressed play. Belinda had given way to "Hit" by The Sugarcubes. It was the band that Bjork was in before she went solo. The lyrics made me smile. I wasn't supposed to have skipped school that day but I did; and my life changed forever. My life changed for the better. I closed my eyes and listened to the music.

Three

Si was waiting outside his building when I turned the corner. His dad's black Jeep Ranger was parked outside. Si looked sweaty and frustrated but his face softened when he saw me walking towards him.

His dad appeared from the entrance and wiped a bit of sweat from his forehead. He smiled when he saw me. "Alright, Lu"

"Alright, Mr. Trelawney." He found it funny the first time I met him that I answered his question. Si hadn't told me that it was a thing in Cornwall to say *Alright?* As a way of greeting someone.

Si gave me a kiss hello on the lips. Mr. Trelawney smiled. He was nice from the moment I met him and treated me like another son. I wondered if my dad would have been the same. My mother treated Si like another son. She treated James and Cuchi like her other children too. Si got his smile from his dad. He was handsome with a boyish charm and he looked after himself. Si joked that he inherited his skincare routine from his dad and not his *mum* as he called her.

"Well that's the last of the boxes, son."

"Thanks dad." Si said.

"Right then. I'll leave you boys to it." Mr. Trelawney gave Si a hug and a kiss on both cheeks like the French do. He had picked that up when he was a young man living in Paris and never lost it. Si only ever did that around his family. It was a side of him that existed at home, in private. His family customs were a mixture of every place they had lived. We both shared that outsider thing of not being like the families on TV. *Maybe that's what made us New Yorkers?*

"Love you dad. Give mum my love."

Mr. Trelawney hugged and kissed me on both cheeks.

"Bye Mr. Trelawney. Say hi to Mrs. Trelawney."

"I will Lu. We're having Sunday lunch at ours. Invite your mum."

Si and I looked at each other. Our parents hadn't met yet as his had spent most of the summer travelling. It was great because it was like we lived alone most of the time. *What if they didn't get along?*

"Sure thing Mr. Trelawney."

He got into his Jeep and drove off. Si and I stood there taking in the invite. It may not had been the best time to mention dinner with my mother but I didn't want to take that upstairs to our place.

"So my mother is coming down to the Village tomorrow for dinner."

Si looked at me a little defeated. "Okay."

I could tell the way he said it, that it wasn't. Si had a way of becoming quiet when something wasn't right or okay. He went to walk away but I grabbed him by the hand.

"Hey, the sooner she sees the place the less she'll say no about me staying. This is a good thing."

He took a deep breath and I could see his shoulders relax. He grabbed my other hand and looked into my eyes. His face softened and his eyes drew me in. They were like topaz, which was my Uncle Jose's birthstone. Si pulled me close and we kissed with tongues and feeling.

"I know you're right baby. That's actually genius."

The way he said *baby* made me melt. It wasn't the playful sound of "baby" the way James said it, which reminded me of Southern church ladies. It was the verbal equivalent of putting his arms around me and pulling me close to him.

We walked into the building and up the stairs into the apartment. Although the room was full of boxes and nothing personal was out yet, I knew I was home. The polished wood floors reflected the exposed brick surrounding the two windows which let in a nice amount of light. Once the trees shed their leaves, I had a feeling that the room would have more natural light which would make those cold months a little brighter. I couldn't wait to see how the leaves changed colors before they fell. The living room had some built in shelves on the wall and a sofa that looked right out of the pages of the LL Bean catalogue. The type of sofa that you pictured in front of a fireplace in Maine or someplace like that. His parents had bought a new one for their country house and given him their old one. To the right was a doorway that led to a narrow kitchen. To the left of the room was another doorway which was the bedroom. I could see the futon Si had picked out a few weeks ago already laid out. I grabbed his hand and led him towards it which reminded me of that Erasure song he had put on the first mix tape he made me.

He had that grin he got when he knew he should be doing one thing but decided to do something else. I pushed him onto the bed and climbed on top of him. I ran my fingers through his hair. His lips tasted a little salty and he smelled of sweat and Speed Stick. I could feel his body squirm under me as I held his hand in mine. There was no better way to celebrate our new home together.

It was about 11pm when we gave up unpacking for the night. The majority of it had been done. The kitchen was in order. The living room had been set up with the stereo, a desk with his new IBM computer. He had one shelf of books as the rest of his collection he decided to keep at his parents because of space. The other shelf had pictures of us from Pride, and hanging out at the piers. There was also a photo of his parents on a bridge in Paris when they were younger. *Si really did take after his dad.*

We made up the bed and decided to leave unpacking the clothes till the morning.

"I'm starving." I rubbed my stomach and it growled.

"Me too. Pizza?"

"Yea. Bleeker?"

"You read my mind." He walked over and kissed me. "Let's go."

Walking down the stairs, we bumped into Roberta who worked the front desk at The Center and spent most of her Saturday's telling us to quiet down. She had a harsh look in her eyes and was prone to moments of softness, though this was not one of them.

"Roberta? I didn't know you lived here." Si Said.

"Oh joy, now you do." She said with no emotion.

We both sort of smiled, not sure if she was being serious or not.

"Alright then." I said.

"Don't be getting ideas about knocking on my door for a cup of sugar now. There's a supermarket three blocks away."

"We won't." Si said.

She stopped before she got to her door and then said. "Welcome to the building kids."

I thought I saw her smile as she opened it.

The light was pouring into the living room when I walked through it to get to the kitchen and make coffee. In a weird way, it felt no different from when we were at his parents. W4th Street and Charles Street was another historic tree lined block and it was quiet. My bedroom in The Bronx didn't face the street but you could always hear music, or the soft hum of traffic. There was always something that reminded you that you were in the city. Not here though, not where his parents lived either.

I put the coffee maker on and then opened the fridge. The only thing in the fridge was a half bottle of Evian water that I am sure his dad had left, the box of pizza from last night with leftovers for breakfast in it and a small carton of half & half. The kitchen filled with the smell of freshly ground hazelnut from McNulty's. I grabbed the bottle of water and took a sip of it as I closed the door. It was then I felt like I was being watched. I had walked from the bedroom to the kitchen naked. I looked out the window and saw a guy sat on his little terrace reading a newspaper shirtless. Although I didn't catch his eye, I could tell by the smile on his face he had seen me. I was embarrassed for a moment and then I looked down at my body. I felt flattered and because he didn't stare or make it obvious, I shrugged and took the compliment. I headed back to our bedroom with the bottle of water in my hand.

Si had just woken up. He saw me, rubbed his eyes and sat up. The blanket rested just above his waist, and he smiled as he stretched his arms.

"Morning."

I handed him the bottle of water and lay down on my stomach. I perched on my elbows and looked at him.

"Good morning."

He sniffed the air. "Is that coffee?"

I nodded. Our eyes met. I pulled myself up and sat across his lap.

"You're amazing."

"So are you." I put my arms around his neck.

He kissed me. We both got a blast of our own bad breath and laughed. We then got out of bed and put our robes on. Si went to the bathroom and I went to the kitchen to pour the coffee which had filled the apartment up with a sweet nutty smell. I poured his into his NYU cup that he always drank his coffee from. Mine was a white cup with the Rainbow flag on it that I had bought at Don't Panic!

He yawned as he walked towards me from the bathroom. I handed him his cup and asked him if he wanted to sit on the fire escape and drink our coffee?"

"Yea that sounds good."

The temperature was perfect as we sat side by side. No chill. No humidity. The street was busy but from the top floor it was far enough away not to distract from the peace. The fire escape had a better view of the terrace across the street. The guy who saw me earlier that morning was still there. He held his coffee cup to us as if he was toasting and smiled. He then took a sip and returned to the *New York Observer,* which was easy to spot because of the pink paper it used. It was also one of the papers that Mrs. Trelawney read.

"A friend?" Si teased as he pressed against my shoulder.

"Possibly more. My friends haven't seen me naked."

"Is that right?"

"We should get some blinds for the windows."

Si laughed. "Bed, Bath and Beyond it is then."

We drank our coffee in a comfortable silence. The world was perfect in that moment. It was peaceful. After coffee, we went back in and finished the pizza from the night before. Leftover cold pizza had become one of my favorite breakfast foods.

Si's cousin Lowena had given his parents some mix tapes she had made for him when they had stopped in London on their way back from Paris, over the summer. They were about the same age and she lived in some place called Camden which Si said was like living in the East Village.

He put one on. The first track was like nothing I had ever heard and the singer's voice was sexy and English. Si started singing along to it as soon as it started.

I loved it when he sang. Even though he never got it right, he lost himself in the music.

"Who's this?" I asked as I felt my body move to the guitars.

"Suede. Animal Nitrate. Like it?"

"I do."

It was catchy and as we unpacked the bedroom, the music continued with bands I had never heard of called Ride, Lush and Blur. *Did all English bans just have one name?* It was funny to think that only earlier that week we were dressed in Belinda Carlisle wigs and now we were listening to *indie* music as it was called.

After unpacking, we showered so we could head to Bed, Bath and Beyond. As we were getting dressed, the intercom rang and we both looked at one another as if we had been caught doing something bad.

Si walked over and answered it.

"Hey Bitches." It was Cuchi.

I laughed and Si rolled his eyes. He left the door open for her as we finished getting dressed.

Cuchi sauntered in with James as I was putting my t-shirt on and my mouth dropped. We had been friends now for about four months and it was only a handful of times I had seen her out of drag in public. I knew that underneath Cuchi was Xavier or Xavy as he preferred to be called. I also knew that whereas Cuchi wore foundation that was a little "cakey" and her lips were always a deep red, Xavy's skin was smooth and mocha with high cheekbones that made him look like he could have been a member of Menudo. What was most striking though was his thick curly black hair that looked like lacquer against his skin tone. Xavy was dressed in blue jeans, a maroon v-neck sweater with a white t-shirt underneath and black shoes. There were traces of Cuchi though in the subtle eyeliner and grin.

"Hey Cuchi." I said and gave her a kiss.

"*Papi,* Cuchi is in the bag." He pointed to the oversized weekend bag he was carrying.

"Sorry. Hey Xavy." I was still learning.

Xavy smiled. "You'll get there honey."

Si came out of the bathroom looking sexy as hell. He had run some water through his hair to make it manageable and it had a wet look to it that made his dirty blonde hair look darker and his brown eyes sparkle.

"Hey Xavy." Si could switch pronouns with ease.

"Cuchi needs to stay in the bag most days." James said and laughed but the comment fell flat as Xavy just glared at him.

"James, don't start." Xavy looked around the room. "Oooh this is cute."

James handed Si a gift bag. "Just a little something to cleanse the new place." He said. "You don't want other people's negativity hanging around."

Si opened the bag and pulled out a large stick of white sage. He then emptied the rest of the bag on the coffee table. There were some rain scented candles, a piece of clear quartz and some moldavite bath salts.

"Thank you." Si had a smile ear to ear as he hugged James.

"You're welcome." James was happy with the response. He was dressed in black jeans, a white turtleneck that hugged his torso and he had a glow about him that I had come to expect.

I walked over to Xavy and put my arm around him. "You okay?"

Xavy went to shrug me off and then stopped. "Just an argument with my mother, *Papi*." He took a deep breath. "The neighbors saw me leaving in drag and you know what *Doña "What are people going to think?"* is like."

I didn't know what to say so I just hugged him.

"Thanks *Papi*." I could see him hold back his emotions. "To make matters worse, *Señorita Esa Cosa."* He looked around the room. "You know my sister Laura." We all sighed. "Went and told our father that it wasn't the first time." Xavy looked away. "I'll get something on that *cabrona*, watch me."

James shook his head. "Gurl, you just a walking *Telemundo* show."

"Telenovela." Si said which made us all look at him. "What? I listen. It is easy to learn another language when you already know more than one."

I blew Si a kiss. Listening to Xavy made me feel very lucky that I had a supportive mother. His parents were conservative. They accepted their gay son because what he did downtown was his business but he was supposed to be "normal" and dress "normal" in their Co-Op. The doormen let Cuchi use the service elevator to sneak in and out but it seems like they found out about that arrangement.

Si gave them both the tour which took less than two minutes and told them we were off to Bed, Bath and Beyond. James looked out the window and waved.

Xavy ran to have a look. "Who's that?"

"That's Chad" James waved. "He's a bartender in the East Village."

"Oh is he? *Sucia.*"

"Gurl, I'm not you." James said. "He comes into the store."

"Oh, one of your New Age queens."

James dismissed Xavy's comment. Over the summer, Carol needed extra staff so he started working at Stick, Stone and Bone.

"You still gonna work there when school starts?" I asked.

"Yea, a few hours after school and when she needs the extra help." James responded. "You still gonna work for Jackie?"

"A couple of afternoons." As much as the money was helpful, it was more about being able to be downtown during the school week. It meant Si and I could sneak some time when our weekday sleepovers ended.

"Right! We ready." Si said. His tone reminded me of a dad rounding up his kids.

"Don't you mean *¿Listos?* Lady Languages." Xavy said.

Si stuck his tongue out at him.

We walked towards 7th Avenue South and crossed onto Greenwich Avenue near Two Boots Pizza. I could feel Fall in the air. In the shade, it was wrap your hand around a coffee weather but in the sun, it felt as if you could get away with shorts and a sweater on top. We passed The Dew Drop Inn and Uncle Charlie's on our way towards Sixth Avenue. When we passed Patchin Place and the Jefferson Market Library, the streets were busier. I loved the way it went from quiet too busy at the turn of a corner. I smiled when I thought back to June and how I wandered into this area lost and was found by Si, Cuchi and James. I took Si's hand and he held it tight.

We walked proud together.

When we crossed 14th Street, we continued walking till we were distracted by the large windows that looked into David Barton Gym.

"I don't get the muscle thing." I said.

"Doesn't do it for me." Si responded and tickled the palm of my hand.

"Oh I see it." James said.

"Mhmm." Xavy added. "Damn baby." He stuck his tongue out at a handsome Asian guy in very revealing shorts and a blue tank top who was lifting weights. The guy smiled back at Xavy and winked.

Not all the guys working out were muscular but looking at them made me feel as if I could work out every day of the week and still never have a body like any of them. Si put both his arms around me and pulled me away.

"You're perfect." He whispered in my ear and kissed me on the cheek.

I giggled. "So are you." I held his arms around me for a moment longer before calling out to Xavy and James that we were walking on.

"We'll catch up." James said.

"Yea…" Xavy trailed off as he blew kisses towards the gym windows.

Si and I continued walking up 6th Avenue. When we got outside Bed, Bath and Beyond, Si had this look in his eyes. He was a kid in a candy store armed with his dad's credit card. I knew how much he was looking forward to furnishing the apartment and even more dangerous, was his love of candles, blankets and soft furnishings in general.

By the time James and Xavy joined us in the store, we were in the checkout line. They helped us carry all the bags and blinds back to *our* place. *That still sounded weird, but nice weird.* Si had gone candle crazy and bought some green and blue bedding which I couldn't wait to put on the bed. He also bought a pull down shade for the bedroom that blocked out light. Something we would need after a night of partying.

"Your dad is going to kill you." I said to him as we walked back.

"Nah." He said. "My mum though." He then winked.

It took us what felt like ages to get back to his. When we got to the outside of his building Xavy put the bags he was carrying down.

"Si, you better have some food in the fridge or something."

"Yes girl, I'm starving." James said.

I looked at Si as my stomach growled. He handed me his wallet and said, "Can you get some pizza baby?"

"Bleeker or Two Boots?"

"I'm not stoned, so Bleeker." Xavy said. "I'll come with you."

We put our bags in the entrance hall for Si and James to carry up and I kissed Si on the lips before we headed out.

Xavy linked his arm with mine as we walked up towards Bleeker Street. He put his head on my shoulder and said, "I love you *Papi*, you know that, right?"

"I love you too." I did. I loved Xavy/ Cuchi. I loved James. I couldn't imagine my life without them or without Si.

When we got to Manatus, I said to Xavy to hold on as I wanted to book a table for dinner. Xavy looked at me.

"Of course you're invited or Cuchi." I smiled.

The host booked us in for 6.30 and took my details. Xavy jumped up and down in excitement.

"Maria's first visit to the Village." He screamed which caused a few people in the restaurant to take notice of us. I pulled him towards the exit before they canceled our reservation.

We headed to the pizza place and waited outside after ordering. It hit me that Xavy was more excited about my mother visiting than I was. I wanted her to see that I was safe. I had no intention of showing her Tiffany's, Fat Cat or the piers. My two worlds were about to meet and the Village would no longer be my secret. Part of me wasn't sure I was ready for that.

When we got back to the apartment, Si and James were listening to "Whatever Lola Wants" and dancing along. Si was unpacking the blinds and James was putting a maroon fluffy blanket on the sofa. We sat on the floor of the living room around the pizza box as if it were a campfire and ate pizza as the music continued from one jazz song to another.

Between the four of us, we put the blinds up after eating pizza. Si made coffee to keep us going and when we were done, the apartment felt like a home, a place to shut the world out.

"If your mother wasn't coming down, I'd say let's smoke up." Xavy said.

I could tell Si and James were tempted. If she hadn't been, I would have jumped at the chance. I wasn't even sure about wanting to do much after the afternoon we'd had. I was tired. I looked around the apartment and saw candles waiting to be lit and a blanket on the sofa waiting to be crawled under. I wanted nothing more than for it to be just the two of us.

"After she leaves." I said to Xavy.

Xavy grabbed his bag and pulled out a half a bottle of Bacardi. He got up and poured a little bit in each of our glasses of Coca-Cola. He raised his glass to the room.

"To your new home." He drank it in one go. "Now bitches, it's time for Cuchi to make an appearance."

"You spill anything in there, you clean it up. This ain't Tiffany's, okay." Si said.

James and I laughed. We were all too familiar with the mess Cuchi could leave but as Xavy pointed out time and time again, Cuchi didn't just happen. Although she looked like she did according to James.

There was a definite feeling of time moving on. That we were hanging out in *our* new place, meant that summer was really behind us. I thought about having to go back to school. About how my world would split again from the freedom of the summer to the anxiety that I felt each day I went to school. I knew it was just one more year but that year already felt like a sentence with no chance of early parole.

My thoughts were interrupted by Si's hand on my shoulder. "You alright?"

He had this way of knowing when my mind was wandering and the gentle tone of his voice pulled me back enough so I wouldn't get too lost.

"What? Yea. Sorry. I was just thinking about how nice this is but how it feels different from the summer."

"What do you mean baby?"

James looked at me as well. He tilted his head to the side as if he was confused but interested.

"Oh, just that the summer was crazy. It felt like we could do what we wanted and now, I don't know. In this apartment. Senior year. You're in your second year." I said, pointing to Si. "Just feels grown up compared to a week ago."

Cuchi poked her head out of the bathroom. She had on her black bobbed wig that she swore made her look like a Puerto Rican flapper girl but was more Martika the way she wore it. She started singing "Seasons Change" by Exposé, which made me laugh and cut the atmosphere I had brought into the room.

"Gurl!" James said. "I keep telling you, lip synch. Lip synch is your talent."

"Mmmmhmmm." Si added.

"*¡Cabrones!*" She closed the bathroom door.

The room was lighter and it made me happy. I put my arms around Si and hugged him. I then walked over to James and gave him a hug.

Four

It felt like the temperature had dropped from earlier that day as we walked towards West 4th Street subway station to pick up my mother. I told her to stay on the D all the way down so she didn't have to change trains. She had beeped me when she left so I knew it was about 40 minutes before she would arrive, give or take.

Cuchi was in an over the shoulder all in one black mini skirt and black stockings. She had forgotten her razor and Si refused to let her use his. Her stiletto heels clacked against the sidewalk as she walked with her arm linked to James. Si and I walked behind them hand in hand.

As we passed Sheridan Square, I had a flashback to when I first walked up that street, past Stonewall to meet Si after he finished work. Another chapter of my life started then; and a new one was beginning as we headed to meet my mother. I squeezed his hand and he smiled at me.

We turned the corner on 6th Avenue and as we approached the station, I could see my mother standing outside The Waverly Movie Theater. She was wearing her black leather jacket that hung around mid-thigh. She had owned that jacket for as long as I could remember. I think it was a gift from my dad. Her hair was pulled back in a bun and she was wearing very light make up. Our eyes met and she smiled. She looked relieved that we had arrived. She disliked downtown at the best of times but she didn't look out of place. Still, downtown was my space, it was Uncle Jose's space. Hers was The Bronx.

I smiled and waved. She waved as she walked towards us. Cuchi whistled and yelled out.

"Arrrrrrrrgh, *¡Mami! ¡Que guapa!*"

People around us looked for a moment before continuing on their way. My mother's cheeks went red. She was smiling though when she got to us.

"*Ay mija, cayate.* Shut up." She put her arms around Cuchi who stood about 3 inches above her.

I watched them hug and it was then I noticed that my mother had a similar look in her eyes when she was around Cuchi that she had when her and Uncle Jose would hang out. They looked like girlfriends ready to tell each other some good gossip.

My mother then turned to James and said, "looking so handsome." She gave him a kiss and a hug.

James smiled from ear to ear.

"Hey mama, you look *fierce* tonight."

My mother snapped her fingers which bordered on cute and then made things awkward by responding, "*Gracias*, Miss Thing!"

I cringed and Si tapped me on the shoulder as if to say *she's trying, leave her alone.*

"*Simon, mi otro hijo.*"

"Hi Mrs Morales." Si still couldn't bring himself to call her Maria and after the first month, she stopped trying to make him. I couldn't bring myself to call his parents Matthew and Susan either. He gave her a kiss on both cheeks like he would his own parents.

"Oh I guess I'm last then." I said, offended.

She looked at me with comical disapproval. *"Mi hijo favorido."*

"Tu unico hijo ma."

Cuchi slapped me on the arm. *"¡Que Vergüenza!* Using the informal. Shame."

As if they had rehearsed the performance my mother said, "I know. I don't know what to do with him."

James and Si laughed and my mother hugged me and she kissed me on the cheek. Less than 5 minutes in the Village and she was cooler than I was after 4 months. She linked one arm around mine and another around Si.

"Where are we eating? I'm starving."

"Manatus." I said.

"Mana-*que?*"

"It's a bit like a better diner." Si said.

"Comida gringa Mami except everyone in the place is gay." Cuchi said. "You bitches really don't know how to just spit it out."

"Oh they prefer it." James said which made Cuchi slap him in the arm. "Ow. Oh, no it's good Maria. You like Meat Loaf or Chicken Parmesan? They do nice plates like that. Burgers too." His attempt at trying to save himself was funny to watch.

"Ma. You want to see the apartment first?"

She nodded. As we walked back, she took in the sights and I watched her as we walked past shops selling sex toys, loud bars and the sounds of the street becoming one murmur. The wonder still got to me. Our neighborhood was pretty much Spanish speaking. Everyone knew one another and at times it felt like a Puerto Rican village had been transplanted from the island, one person at a time.

When we walked by The Monster, she said. "Jose used to tell me about that place. It's where the older men like the younger men. *¿No?*" The way she said it, made us all smile.

We crossed towards Riviera and my mother stopped in her tracks. "*¿Este es el* Tiffany's?* She asked. "*Ay* the stories he used to tell me about that place."

"Oh *Mami*, the stories that still happen there." Cuchi added.

It took me coming out and Si moving to the Village to get my mother to come down and I could see in her eyes that she wished she had come down with my Uncle, when he was still alive. I felt his presence whenever I walked around the Village. I felt like he watched over me, and now us. A larger than life angel with rainbow wings and a Newport in one hand.

We continued on walking. When we got to the apartment, she walked around like an inspector. She kept looking at us and then around as if she were searching for a hidden chamber or a sign that it was unsafe. It took me a moment to realize she was doing it as a joke to tease Si. She succeeded to my amusement, and hers.

"Luis, sleeps on the sofa right?"

Si looked at me, then at my mother, then back at me.

Cuchi and James were suppressing their laughter through strained faces.

"Ma, you told me never to lie to you."

Si froze and turned red.

My mother smiled and patted him on the arm. "*Mijo*, I'm just fucking with you."

Cuchi and James let out their laugh and Si realized he had been set up. He relaxed and tried to go along with the joke at his expense. I could feel his heart racing as I gave him a hug to comfort him. He was still unsure of her humor and I suspected it had to do with her accent. She had lived in The Bronx since she was 18 when her and my dad moved from Aguadilla in the early 70's but she never lost her accent and though she never spoke *Spanglish* at work, it became her default in the rest of her life.

She walked towards the door. "*Vamanos*, I'm starving."

Cuchi and James followed her. Si and I were alone for the first time since that morning. He held me in his arms and looked into my eyes.

"I can't wait till it's just you and I later."

"Me too."

He kissed me on the lips and as much as I wanted to take him into the bedroom right then and there, we followed the rest of them down.

Manatus was busy when we got there so I was happy I had made a reservation. Stepping inside of it was like taking a step back in time. The bar that stuck out from the side of the entrance reminded me of those old fashioned donut places where bored waitresses rolled their eyes at customers. The host sat us towards the patio doors. It was one of the other things I loved about the Village. There were these hidden spaces behind buildings you walked past and paid no mind to; like Espresso Bar.

The waiter introduced himself as Marty. He had been our waiter before and always looked happy to see us. He was older than the rest and I always thought if you sat him down, he probably had some stories to tell about the Village. We were on better behavior in Manatus than we usually were at Tiffany's but the other staff seemed to watch us as if we were going to ruin the ambiance. I introduced him to my mother and he bowed his head as if he had met someone important.

"Glass of wine Madame?"

"So fancy." She said which made him smile. "A red, please."

"Excellent." He then looked at the rest of us. "2 iced teas, 2 cokes?"

My shoulders relaxed and I felt silly for being nervous about her visit. I remembered how nervous I was the first time we all had dinner at *El Chino*. It was the first time I had met Xavy who had he not arrived with James, I would have walked past.

"Shady bitch, I don't look that different." He said to me as he slapped me on the arm.

Like then I was afraid that if she didn't approve, then she wouldn't let me hang out down in the Village or with my friends. Although we had a good relationship and I loved our time, my world was small. I spent a lot of time alone hoping that one day I would find a place to fit in. That I would meet people who didn't want to hurt me. That I would meet people like me. I felt Si put his hand on my knee and I turned to see him looking at me as if I was the only person in the room. *How did he always know the right thing to do?*

Seeing her talk to Cuchi and James now, it was obvious that she would get along with them. She got along with everyone. Everyone got along with her. She had that confidence that I lacked when talking to others.

"I told you it wouldn't be that bad." I said to Si.

"I never said it would be." He bumped his shoulder against mine in that playful way of ours.

"You didn't have to."

I knew that he wanted the weekend just he and I, but that was because I did too.

Marty returned with our drinks and took our orders. After he left the table, my mother proposed a toast.

"*¡A la familia!*" She said as she looked at each one of us.

We all responded with the same words, apart from Cuchi.

"*Así es.* That's it *Mami.¡Wepa!*" She said.

My mother then said *¡Wepa!* and we joined in.

"I sometimes think I should switch my major to Spanish." Si said. He had picked up bits of Spanish around us over the summer but I wasn't sure that slang words would count towards a degree.

James asked Si about his first week of classes and I watched as my mother and Cuchi had a private moment. It was as if they had stepped into a glass confessional. I watched my mother wipe a tear from Cuchi's eye and give her a big hug. I didn't need to hear the entire conversation. I knew they were talking about Cuchi's fight with her parents. When she let her go, I caught the last thing she said.

"*No llores mi amor.* Don't cry." My mother said. "You have to make them understand. *No hay nada.* There is nothing wrong with you."

Cuchi looked at me, holding up a small drop of mascara from her left eye. "You're so lucky to have huh as your mother."

"Thank you." I was grateful that she had embraced me, and my life in the way she did.

My mother put one hand on Cuchi's shoulder. She looked at James and Si.

"*Mijos,* all of you have a place in my house, at my table, *siempre.* Always. *Cualquiera* cosa. Whatever you need, you ask. If I can, I will. You are all my children and I know that this one." She said as she pointed to me. "*Mi Vida, este aqui* is always safe when he is with you. I don't worry."

James and Cuchi both had tears in their eyes and Si looked as if he was overcome with love.

"Anyway, I love you all." She finished and raised her glass to us all.

Cuchi hugged her and James and Si followed. Cuchi then excused herself to the bathroom to fix her face. I got up after everyone else and put my arms around her. She held my forearms and I kissed her on the cheek and said *"I love you Ma."* She smiled and I could smell the slightest hint of Giorgio Beverly Hills. I never noticed before that she wore perfume or maybe she had worn it just for the night. *I guess we were both still learning things about each other.*

By the time Cuchi came back with her makeup intact, the food had arrived. My mother enjoyed her Chicken Parmesan. I was pretty sure she was the only straight person in the restaurant and yet she didn't look out of place. She had another glass of wine and we finished the meal off with some New York Cheesecake.

"This was your *Papa's* favorite." She said.

"I didn't know that."

"You never asked."

That was true. I never asked anything about my father. Carlos was just a name on my birth certificate and a guy in a few framed photos my mother kept on her dresser. Uncle Jose was my stand in dad. He even tried to teach me baseball which he was surprisingly good at and was my dad's favorite sport. I never thought much of Carlos but now we shared a favorite dessert.

"That's cool." Si said. He loved hearing things like that. Like James, he too had a thing about connections in life. There were no coincidences and things mattered. "Oh Mrs. Morales, my parents would like you to join us for Sunday lunch."

She looked at me for reassurance and I smiled back. "I would love to."

I wasn't nervous about her meeting Mr. Trelawney but I did wonder how she and Mrs. Trelawney would get along. It wasn't that she wasn't a nice person. She was. It was that they came from such different backgrounds and Mrs. Trelawney could come across as cold and distant when she wasn't sure how to connect with a person. I found that out on our first meeting until I noticed she was reading James Baldwin's *Notes on a Native Son* and I mentioned how much I enjoyed *Giovanni's Room*. I put it out of my head for the night. I was sure the meal would be fun for all of us.

We all pitched in to pay for the meal as a treat to my mother who refused three times before allowing us to.

On the walk back to the station, I was sad to see her go.

She kissed each one of us and gave us big hugs. We had to pry Cuchi off her who kept saying "I love huh so much."

"See you Sunday Simon and we talk about that thing, ok?" She said.

"Ma, I know."

"Know what?" She was intent on keeping up the surprise birthday.

"Call me tomorrow *mijo. Dios de bendigan.*"

We watched her disappear into the station. The sidewalk became crowded as the movie theater let out. There were yellow taxis bumper to bumper. It was a Friday night and it felt like everyone in the city was downtown.

"What shall we do ladies?" Cuchi asked.

We decided against going down to the piers as the temperature had dropped. Si suggested Uncle Charlie's because he knew one of the bartenders who worked there. Christian was cool with us going in as long as we ordered more soft drinks than alcohol and weren't too obvious.

When I got my first fake ID from a shop on 8th Avenue near Port Authority, I hated using it. It cost me $20 and looked handmade.

What became obvious though was that most bars and clubs didn't care as long as they saw some form of ID and once you got to know the staff, as long as you didn't cause any trouble, they didn't care. It was an unspoken rule on the gay scene that made you feel like you were a member of a secret club. I was happy when we got to the entrance that there was no bouncer on the door.

The bar was busy but not crowded when we walked in and the video screens were playing "So Many Men." There were people moving along to the music. Christian saw Si and winked at him. We made our way to the end of the bar where we ordered some drinks.

Cuchi was dancing around and attracting attention which made me nervous. James grabbed a handful of free entry flyers for Limelight since his contact only got him guest list for Saturday not Friday, although he was working on changing that. We stood against the back corner and I found myself sinking into Si. I didn't feel tired. I just felt like I wanted to be anywhere but there even though the atmosphere was fun.

I looked over towards the bar and James was talking to some guy in a suit. The guy looked like he smelled of Ralph Lauren Polo and worked in a skyscraper.

"His wife's probably in the Hamptons." Cuchi said to us. "*Pobrecita.*"

"Or boyfriend." Si added.

"Mhmm." Cuchi responded. She took a sip from her Diet Coke. "Ugh, I need to spice this shit up." She reached into her purse and pulled out a small bottle of Malibu and poured it into her drink. She then waved it us as an offer.

Si looked around as if we were being watched. I looked towards the bar but the staff were distracted by most of the bar singing along to "It's Raining Men." James joined us and the suit guy was nowhere to be seen.

Cuchi took a sip of her drink and looked at James. "Where's your benefactor?"

"Oh gurl, envy doesn't match that outfit."

Cuchi looked away pretending to be offended and then they looked at each other and laughed. It was going to be one of those nights for the double act. I finished my coke and yawned.

I leaned into Si and said "Can we go home?"

"Absolutely." He smiled and then kissed me on the head.

We left Uncle Charlie's and although they said they were okay with it, I could tell that James and Cuchi were disappointed we weren't staying out with them. Si took my hand as soon as we left and the bouncer who had just taken his place, wished us a good night and "to stay safe, boys"

The city was ready to party with people going to and from bars and restaurants. Taxi drivers were honking and yelling at each other to "get out of the way." I was feeling the opposite. I was looking forward to being *home* in a few minutes time and shutting the world out. Just the two of us, alone in *our* space.

As we walked hand in hand, the city felt like it was ours. I felt that sense of home even more now that my mother had become a part of it. Si yawned and I followed.

We ran into Roberta on the way into the building. She was dressed ready to party without a hair out of place.

"Hey kids." She said.

"Hey honey." Si responded.

"Not going out tonight?"

"We're tired." I said.

"Nice to have someone to be tired with." She winked and smiled.

I saw her turn the corner and head towards 7th Avenue South.

Five

I woke up to the smell of hazelnut coffee and eggs cooking. I looked around the room in a moment of confusion. I was still getting used to being in the new apartment. I looked at the dresser and noticed something that Si must have put up while I was sleeping.

It was a photo that Jackie had taken of us without our knowledge. It was my first week of work and Si had come to pick me up so we could go to the movies. Our eyes met as I was tidying up the dinner table that doubled as my desk. She captured that moment in black and white. I didn't even know about it until I mentioned in conversation to Jackie that I didn't know what to get him for our two monthiversary. I bought an 8 x 10 silver photo frame for it. Si was speechless when he opened the box.

I got up and put my grey robe on and went out towards the kitchen. He had the stereo on low and was singing along to Pixie's "Gigantic" trying to hit the high notes. I watched him for a moment as he sang at the eggs. Whenever Si thought no one was looking, he would let go. I found myself falling for him all over again as I watched him.

He turned around and saw me but instead of blushing, he turned the stove off and danced his way towards me. He grabbed me by the waist and moved me along to the music with him. I didn't know who Pixies were a few months ago but they had become one of the many bands that we shared, like Belinda Carlisle but probably cooler sounding to most other people. To us though, it was just *us*. Not getting hung up on the latest thing was something that was very much *us*.

I kissed him on the lips. "What's for breakfast?"

"Omelettes and coffee." He continued to move his body against me.

"Perfect."

I looked at the clock and it was 8.20am. It was strange and nice to be up that early on a Saturday and not have a sore head from Limelight. All summer long, we barely got out of bed before noon to order food from the deli around the corner or heading to The Village Star for a bite to eat before BiGLYNY.

I sat down at the table and he brought breakfast out. He even put a sprig of parsley on the omelette like they did in diners. I cut it in half and I could see green peppers and ham covered in cheese ooze out. I took a bite and tasted the mixture of provolone and cheddar.

"Mmm, like Tiffany's never made." I said.

He winked.

There was something so grown up about being in our own space. It felt a bit like playing adult which was different from the summer when it felt like we were two kids left alone at his parent's house.

"What do you want to do this morning?" Si asked after taking a sip of coffee.

I looked behind at the window. The sky was blue and I had never been in the Village that early after a restful sleep.

"You want to go for a walk?"

"Sounds good." He blew me a kiss.

We finished our breakfast and I washed the dishes as Si took a shower. I opened the kitchen blinds all the way and looked outside the window. The guy from across the street was not on his terrace but his calico cat was. It was on the ledge looking as if it owned the world and it wanted you to make sure you knew it. I smiled at the cat who then lifted his leg and started to clean himself.

After I finished the dishes, I went to the bathroom. Si was brushing his teeth as I took my robe off and stepped into the bathtub. He had left the shower running and he stopped brushing as he looked at me step under the water. When I finished, he was there holding a towel. He had gotten dressed in the time that I showered. He was wearing blue jeans, a black long sleeved shirt with green and red tribal like swirls and his trusty Converse sneakers. He looked like one of those skater boys who hung around Washington Square Park.

"Thanks." I said.

I dried off and got dressed. I picked out black jeans, a green t-shirt and a black zip up of Si's that I had taken to wearing. It smelled of Calvin Klein's Eternity which he had started wearing over the summer. I put a tiny bit of gel in my hair to spike it up. I had never used hair products before I came out and I didn't even know if I had a style or one suited me but I enjoyed mixing things up even if I got it wrong most days.

"You look cute." Si said from the doorway. Given the look in his eyes, I had gotten it right.

"Thanks." I looked down at the floor all shy and then up at him.

"You look hot."

He reached out for me and pulled me towards him. "We look hot." He then kissed me on the neck in that way that made me not want to go out for a walk.

It was a little warmer than I had expected when we left the building so I tied the zip up around my waist which gave me a sort of grunge look. Something that we were seeing more of since that Seattle music was so popular. Si took my hand as we walked up West 4th Street which was peaceful with the sound of birds chirping. We headed towards Espresso Bar to grab a coffee to go.

Lemal was working and greeted us both with kisses and a hug. I remembered how scary I first thought he was and the whole café. Awkward Lu surrounded by all those gorgeous men who now knew my name and liked me. It was still weird.

We left Espresso Bar with our large hazelnut coffees in our hands and headed towards 7th Avenue South. We walked past Caliente Cab Co. and Fudruckers as we headed in the direction of SoHo. It wasn't like we had a destination in mind although we did window shop in the overpriced shops of SoHo before stopping at Dean & Deluca for another cup of coffee and walking up Lafayette towards Astor Place.

Si stopped in front of Colonnade Row and put his arm around me. What was left of it, felt like a bit of Europe frozen in New York. It was dirty with soot but that only added to its majesty. The columns made me think about how this part of the city really did resemble a village before the warehouses took over which seem to give way to artist's lofts. Through his eyes, I began to see things in the city that I had walked past and didn't take any notice of. Our walks had become as much a part of our relationship as dinner with my mother and hanging out with our BiGLYNY friends.

Before heading back towards the West Village, we walked down St Mark's Place to Kim's Video. Si wanted to rent *Indochine* with his favorite French actress Catherine Denueve. I had only watched a few French films with him and the subtitles meant that we had to watch them more than once for me to understand the whole film but he was happy with that. As a trade off, he also rented Almodóvar's *Women on the Edge of a Nervous Breakdown* so he had to read subtitles.

We stopped off at Papaya King for a couple of hot dogs and a drink before walking up to The Center. Halfway down Greenwich Avenue, he took my hand in his and we swung them like little kids playing. It was a great start to the day and we got to The Center before everyone else. We sat on the stoop, me between his legs and his arms around me. We shared a cigarette as the sun beamed down on us. It was a peaceful moment that didn't last very long.

"Ey *Papi.*" Cuchi looked as if she had slept on the street and smelled of it too.

"Gurl." I said. "What happened?"

"Ugh, don't ask."

Si and I looked at each other.

"Where's James?" Si asked.

"He should be here any minute. He left the club before me."

"Did you go home?" I asked.

She looked the other way before looking me in the eye. She didn't have to answer. The argument with her mother had left a mark and I was annoyed that she hadn't called us. The thought of her out there on her own on the streets gave me a chill. She had warned me from day one the dangers of being young and gay in the city. I looked at Si.

He put his arm around her. "C'mon."

"Where are we going?"

"You're having a shower." We looped our arms to hers and walked in the direction of Eighth Avenue. Most of the group approached The Center from 7th Avenue South so to avoid them we walked the long way back to our apartment.

Cuchi was silent the entire way and I thought about the words she first said to me when we met. "*Familia.* Family. We look out for each other."

Si made a pot of coffee while I got Cuchi a spare towel. She mumbled a low *thank you* before closing the bathroom door.

"I don't know what to say." I said to Si.

"It's tough. If she needs to crash here tonight, we have a sofa."

"You're a great guy, you know that." I said to him. I knew he wanted to chill that night with some videos.

He smiled and put his arms around me. "We take care of each other."

Xavy appeared with a towel wrapped around his waist. He looked more alive than Cuchi did. Si poured him a cup of coffee and handed it to him.

"Thank you honey."

"Feel better?"

Xavy waved me off. "Yea, I'm fine. Thank you."

"Do you want to call your mother?"

He gave me a *why bitch?* Look.

"Do you want to call *my* mother?"

It was a silly comment but it made us all laugh. My pager buzzed and I recognized the number from the pay phone in The Center. I knew it was most likely James who was probably wondering where we all were.

"Can I borrow some clothes?" Xavy asked.

"Underwear too?" Si said.

"Oh honey, I don't wear underwear."

"Easy access?" I said.

Xavy mouthed *fuck you* in response. I lead him to the bedroom and pulled out some clothes for him to wear.

We headed back after Xavy changed. James was sat outside The Center with Casey smoking a cigarette. She looked as if she wasn't ready to give up on summer as she was dressed in her cut off jeans, boots, a black tank top and flannel shirt wrapped around her waist. Her hair was tied in a perfect bun.

"Hey ladies." She said as she saw us. She gave us each a mama bear hug.

"Where have you three been?" James said. He looked at our faces as if he was trying to get answers from our expressions.

"Okaaaay." Casey said. "See you inside?" She made her exit aware that we needed a moment.

"Someone didn't make it home last night and needed a shower." Si said as he tilted his head towards Xavy.

"Oooooh." James smiled.

"Gurl, it wasn't like that. My ass slept in a booth at Tiffany's."

James got up and hugged Xavy. I could see Xavy hold him back tight. I thought I heard James say "you should've called me" but I wasn't sure. It was our turn to let them have their moment.

"C'mon." I said to Si and grabbed his hand.

We walked past a few members of SAGE (Senior Action in a Gay Environment) who were in the courtyard with cups of coffee. They smiled and waved as we walked by. Both of us smiled and waved back.

We entered the room and the group was already sat in a circle. Si and I grabbed two chairs and sat next to Casey who had made some space for us in the circle. There were a few new faces and some people who I had not seen in a few weeks because of end of summer vacation and all that stuff.

James and Xavy walked in just as the meeting was being called to order.

"Sorry everybody. Cuchi made me late." Xavy said. Most of the room laughed but a few people looked confused. Inside jokes were very popular in the group but it didn't take long to be let in on them.

We went around the room as usual. There was a new guy who was sort of half looking at Si and me and then looking away. Some of the guys in the group including Xavy had taken notice of him. He had dark brown hair, dark eyes and wore Cavaricci jeans like the guys in my high school. He had that *Guido* look that would have made me cross the street if I had seen him in The Bronx but at The Center, he didn't pose a threat. The whole room leaned in when it was his turn.

"Hi. I'm Rafa or Rafael, whichever. I'm from City Island. It's my first time here and I like boys and girls so I guess I'm bi. Anyway, hello."

He sounded so confident compared to how I sounded when I first attended a meeting. Xavy hung on his every word and given how Cuchi looked earlier that day, it was nice to see Xavy with a smile on his face.

Si and I both looked at them and then smiled at one another.

Six

When I got up to use the bathroom, the world was spinning. It was a stupid idea to go to Limelight the night before our parents were going to meet for the first time. It didn't seem like a stupid idea at the time though. We were all hanging out on the pier like we always did. Xavy was hitting it off with Rafa who everyone had backed off of when they saw the two of them together. Si and I were at the edge of the pier, our legs were hanging off the side and he had his arms around me with his chin on my shoulder when he whispered, "we don't have to watch videos tonight."

That was it.

Next thing I knew we were bypassing the line at Limelight and dancing under hanging cages as techno and lazers lit up the cavernous main room. At least, we hadn't taken any drugs. I regretted the four screwdrivers though.

I was about to get back into bed when my pager went off. I found my jeans near the bedroom door. When I pulled it out to check the number, my eyes widened in a panic.

It was my mother.

"Hey. We need to get up." I patted him awake.

"Huh…What?" He then grabbed me by the arm to pull me back into bed. I let myself fall on top of him and I wanted nothing more than to feel his bare skin against mine for the rest of the day. My pager buzzed again.

"C'mon." I said as I got back up and pulled him with me.

"No fun!"

"Fine then, don't shower with me."

His face lit up and he took my hand as we went to the bathroom. I should have called my mother first but we got swept in the moment.

After showering, I phoned her back as Si got dressed.

"*Mijo*, what took you so long?"

"You don't want to know."

"*Ay Luis*, don't get smart with me."

We agreed to meet her outside the 81st street subway station near the Hayden Planetarium and walk up to Si's parent's house on 79th Street together. We grabbed a greasy ham, egg and cheese sandwich on the way to the subway. The fresh air was helping me wake up and although it was partly cloudy, the sunlight made the sky light up as if it were one of those old paintings that hung in The Met. I wished we had had more time to enjoy the outdoors. I had this dreaded feeling in my stomach because I knew I had to go home to The Bronx that night. I knew that it was the last day before things changed because of school. I knew that we wouldn't be able to spend another night together till at least my birthday. The thought lingered as if it were waiting outside the door and I didn't want to answer it, although it kept ringing the bell.

My mother was outside the gate that led to the Planetarium when we arrived. She was dressed in a flowing black dress and a cream blouse that brought out the honey tones in her skin. She was holding a bouquet of flowers, the kind that came from an actual florist and not the supermarket. She smiled when she saw us.

"*Mijos.*" She gave us both hugs and kisses. I offered to carry the flowers and Si linked his arm around hers as we walked towards Columbus Avenue before taking a left towards his parent's block. For the second time that weekend, my mother was in *my* world and it didn't feel as strange as I thought it would.

When we turned onto 79th Street, she stopped for a moment.

"*¡Que lindo!* How pretty?" She said.

It was one of those typical streets on the Upper West Side with brownstones and trees. We walked halfway down to where his parent's lived. My mother went to climb the stoop to go through the front door but Si guided her to the lower entrance.

"This way Mrs. Morales."

As we walked into the kitchen, my senses went into overload as I took in the smell of rosemary, garlic, and roast beef. I could feel my mouth water as my stomach growled. I saw Mr. Trelawney pull out a large dish with what looked like foil wrapped meat. He put it on the side and looked very pleased with himself.

"Alright Dad." Si said.

He looked up and smiled. "Alright Son. Alright Lu." He rinsed his hand and then turned to my mother. "You must be Mrs. Morales."

"Mrs. Morales, my Dad Matthew."

"Maria, please?"

Mr. Trelawney shook my mother's hand. "*Mucho gusto Maria.*"

My mother smiled. "Ahh *que bueno, habla español.*" She looked around the kitchen like she was on a game show.

"*Un pocito.*"

"Oh Matthew! Stop embarrassing yourself." Mrs. Trelawney entered the kitchen through the stairs leading up to the rest of the house. She was dressed in a simple black dress with a powder blue scarf tied around her neck. I was used to seeing her dressed in her business suit which made her look harsher but as a literary agent, that was her job.

Mr. Trelawney grabbed her by the waist which made her blush. It was obvious where Si got his affectionate manners from.

"Maria, this is my wife Susan."

Mrs. Trelawney and my mother shook hands. She then gave both Si and I hugs.

"It smells really good." I said.

"Ever have a Sunday roast, Lu?"

I shook my head.

"Well you're in for a treat." He said and winked at me. Mr. Trelawney had such a soft and sweet manner that it was hard to imagine him working as a Litigator. According to Si, if you had ever heard his parents argue, you wouldn't be that surprised.

"It's Dad's signature meal." Si said.

"Simon, it's your father's ONLY dish." Mrs. Trelawney said as she poured red wine into some glasses for all of us. Si grabbed the two that were half full for us. His parents were very European about drinking with dinner. My mother allowed me a glass of wine with

Christmas dinner but that was it. I went to the fridge and took out the pitcher of iced tea. I poured Si and I some to go with our dinner.

"So what is a Sunday Roast?" My mother asked.

"A lot of food swimming in brown gravy." Mrs. Trelawney said as she took a sip of wine. She had a teasing grin on her face.

"Never gets old Susan." Mr. Trelawney rolled his eyes. "Well Maria, we have here the most tender roast beef you will ever taste in your life, roasted rosemary and garlic potatoes, honey and mustard parsnips, cauliflower cheese, cabbage, leeks, sugar carrots, peas, Yorkshire puddings all topped with homemade gravy." He then blew Mrs. Trelawney a kiss.

My mother had a look on her face like she was trying to process what he had just said to her but all she could hear were words that made no sense to her. She smiled. "I have never heard of this so I look forward to trying it."

Mrs. Trelawney walked over to my mother and put her hand on her shoulder. "Don't worry Maria. I tease him but it's delicious and Matthew is a fantastic cook."

"Yes Mrs. Morales." Si said. "He really is."

The table was already set and Mr. Trelawney was making space on the kitchen counter for the various dishes he was serving up. My mother pointed to the patio doors and asked what was out there.

"Go ahead and show your mother." Mrs. Trelawney said. "Simon, help me get the condiments for the table."

I guided my mother to the doors and we stepped out into what felt like another world. Hidden behind the brownstones was a patchwork of gardens and patios under large trees that made the air feel a few degrees cooler. The Trelawney's patch was a nice size with room for a table and four chairs, some rose bushes and a bird bath.

"Wow." My mother said.

"*Increíble ¿No?*"

My mother took it all in. "*Maravillosa.*"

You couldn't hear any city noise and it hit me that I couldn't remember the last time it was just her and I. I put my arm around her.

She held my hand and then looked at me. "Okay, what?"

"What do you mean?" I said.

She gave me a half smile. There was no use in trying to fool her.

"Can I stay out a little late tonight?"

"I want you home by 9. You have school tomorrow."

I kissed her on the cheek. "Thank you."

She put her arm around my waist. "*Venga*, let's go in."

When we walked back in, Mr. Trelawney was standing by the counter ready to serve us all. My mother surprised me by having a bit of everything. Apart from Chinese food, pizza and the occasional pasta, I had only ever seen her eat Puerto Rican food. He served Mrs. Trelawney next and then us before he served himself.

As we sat down, I whispered to Si. "I have to be home by 9 tonight."

He smiled and pressed his knee against mine. It meant we could have some time to chill him and me before I had to go home. I wasn't looking forward to sleeping alone and waking up without him by my side but at least, it wouldn't feel as long as it could have felt.

Mr. Trelawney sat down at the head of the table and proposed a toast.

"Maria, *¡Bienvenidos!* Welcome! Thank you for being here." He raised his glass a little higher. "To friends and family."

I saw Mrs. Trelawney smile at Mr. Trelawney like she was seeing him for the first time again. It was beautiful and it reminded me of how Si could look at times. They could both make you feel like you were the only person in the room. Mr. Trelawney winked at her and she blushed.

"Thank you for inviting me Matthew and Susan." My mother said. "*¡Salud!*

"*¡Salud!* We all responded in unison.

I looked at Si. The meal was going well. Our parents were getting along and we had some extra time to look forward to.

Mr. Trelawney insisted I try some horseradish with the meat. It was a bit spicy but with the tender meat, it melted in my mouth. It tasted like perfection. Si had a big spoonful on his plate which he spread around he slices of beef visible through the gravy.

"This is so good Dad." Si said after swallowing a forkful of food.

"Thanks Son."

"So you have this every Sunday?" My mother asked.

"Traditionally in the winter or when it gets cold."Mr. Trelawney said. "But this is isn't my mother's roast. Over the years I added my own touches to it."

"You mean flavor." Si said.

"Simon. That's no way to speak about your Nana's cooking."

"Oh Matthew, she can cook a pasty. I'll give her that." Mrs. Trelawney said. "What would you traditionally have Maria?"

"In Puerto Rico? We have a *sancocho*. It's like a stew." My mother responded.

"Maybe you can make it for us one day." Mr. Trelawney said. He seemed happy the conversation had moved on from criticizing his mother's cooking.

"Of course." My mother said. "I would love it." She enjoyed cooking for others and even when it was just the two of us, she always cooked enough for leftovers. The last time we had dinner with my mother in The Bronx, she sent Si home with two containers full of rice, beans and *carne guisada*. He looked like a kid on Christmas morning when she gave him the bag with the food to take home.

I didn't think it was possible to have that many flavors on one plate but Mr. Trelawney had succeeded. Given the size of the portions, I was pretty sure I wouldn't need to eat later that day.

"Can you cook this?" I said to Si.

Si looked up from his plate and seemed a bit put on the spot. "Um for you? Sure." He then looked at his dad.

Mr. Trelawney looked at Si. "I'll show you whenever you want." You could tell he was excited about passing down the recipe to Si.

"Simon has always loved spending time with his Father." Mrs. Trelawney said and then took a sip of wine. Her words left a heaviness in the room and my mother looked at me unsure of where else to look.

Si looked at his mother and took a sip of wine.

"It's nice to spend time with the kids, no?" They grow up so fast right Susan?" My mother said.

She smiled at my mother. It was a friendly smile and it broke the tension. "They do Maria. They certainly do."

"So when did Si tell you he was gay?" My mother asked which brought the table to a standstill.

"Ma!" I said.

Mr. Trelawney let out a laugh and Mrs. Trelawney followed. Si looked at them both with disbelief. I was curious as Si never spoke about his coming out. He didn't speak much about his life before we met. I hadn't thought about that before my mother asked the question.

"Matthew would you like to answer that?"

He took a sip of wine. "No my lovely, you tell it much better."

Si shook his head and both my mother and myself leant in as if we were about to hear some juicy gossip.

Mrs. Trelawney leaned in and rested her elbows on the edge of table. "It was the start of his senior year at the Lycée. He came home and kept talking about some girl named Erica. Oh what was her name? Her father worked at the Belgian Mission to the UN or something."

"Erica Vanderhoop." Si said with a defeated tone.

"That's right." Mrs. Trelawney continued. "She was a gorgeous girl. I had suspected Simon might be gay when he was a young boy.

He loved singing Belinda Carlisle songs way *too* much for a boy his age"

"Still do!" Si said and shrugged.

I looked at my mother who was listening intently. I pressed my knee against Si's and he pressed back.

"So a few months go by." She took another sip of wine. "When I noticed there were some magazines sticking out from under his mattress. Not dirty ones though, they were *International Male* catalogues." She looked at Si who was turning red. "I put them back and didn't think anything else about it. Matthew can you pour me some more wine." She tapped her glass.

"Haven't you had enough Mum?" Si said.

"Oh Simon, lighten up." Mr. Trelawney got up, walked over and poured some more wine in everyone's glass.

"Thank you darling." She then blew Si a maternal kiss. "The following day we were having brunch at Sarabeth's and this striking boy about Si's age says hello. When I say striking he was the male version of Erica. Simon grudgingly introduced him to us as Eric, Erica's twin brother who he failed to mention at all."

Si was looking down at the table and I squeezed his knee. He put his hand on mine.

Mrs. Trelawney continued on with her story. "So as soon as Eric leaves, I look at Matthew and he looks at Simon. I put my hand on Simon's hand and say to him that I found the magazines. Simon nearly jumps out of his chair and says the *Playgirls??* I look at Matthew who starts laughing and then I respond, no, the *International*

Male catalogues."

Si starts to laugh. "I was such a dork. Anyway Mum, can I finish it since you've embarrassed me enough?"

Mrs. Trelawney took a sip of wine and gestured to Si to continue.

"So after that I told them the truth. I had been involved with Eric not his sister but we covered for one another because Erica was a lesbian and involved with Audrey, a French girl in our school."

"Wow." My mother said. "The lies these kids tell because they are scared." She then took a sip of wine as if she needed to clear her throat.

"Not everyone is as lucky as these two." Mr. Trelawney said.

"So what happened to Eric?" I asked.

Si looked at me. "Um, he went back to Belgium after we graduated."

"Don't worry Lu. He never looked at Eric the way he looks at you."

Si looked at me and smiled. I felt like a dork for asking the question.

"Right then." Susan said. "Who's ready for dessert?"

There were nods of agreement all around the table.

"Simon can you help me please?"

"Sure." Si got up from the table.

Mr. Trelawney started to clear the table and I got up to help him. My mother then joined and the two of us finished the table while Mr. Trelawney set the coffee machine. I piled the plates on the kitchen counter and could hear Si and his mother talking in a heated tone in

French. Si caught my eye and then said something which made his mother look at me and then at him.

I then heard her say. "Simon. We'll talk later."

"Whatever." Si said as he walked towards me with two plates of cheesecake.

"Everything ok?"

"Yea. Just some school stuff."

I had a feeling though it was more than school related by how quiet he became. I put my arm on his shoulder and he flashed me a look that said *thank you.*

Mrs. Trelawney followed with two more plates and Mr. Trelawney grabbed the last plate. He asked me to get some ice cream from the freezer. The smell of coffee filled the kitchen and it hit me how tired I was. I didn't want to waste the few hours I had with Si so I hoped that the cake and the coffee, would help boost my energy levels. After putting the ice cream on the table, I helped Mr. Trelawney with the coffee cups and then we sat down to have dessert.

"This is very good Susan." My mother said after tasting the cake. She then took a sip of coffee which she was less impressed with but anything less than Cafe Bustelo disappointed her. It wasn't obvious to anyone else but I could tell from her mouth movement.

"Thank you Maria." Mrs. Trelawney said.

"What Mum lacks in cooking she makes up in baking."

Mrs. Trelawney ignored Si's comment and looked at me. "Lu, I'm really sorry but we're not going to be able to make it on Friday so I hope it is okay to give you your gift now."

Mr. Trelawney dropped his fork. "We're not."

"No Matthew. Do you not remember that Hervé and Marguerite are in from Paris? We have dinner plans with them?"

"Oh. Right." He looked upset and for the second time that afternoon, the air had become a bit thick. "Maybe after dinner?"

Mrs. Trelawney half smiled back at him. "Well I suppose that's a possibility." She then turned to me with a very warm look on her face and handed me a textured envelope.

"Thank you." I said. I opened the envelope and took out an expensive looking card. It was on thick paper and embossed with gold and maroon letters. There was an image of one of those old fashioned pens with a feather and it said "We write our own stories." Inside in handwriting that was similar to Si's but more slanted was written: *Happy Birthday Lu. Here is a little something to help you start your own library.* In the card was a $100 gift certificate to Shakespeare & Co.

Si looked at his mother. "How personal?"

Mr. Trelawney and I threw him dirty looks. I didn't like that he had decided to take away the moment from me when I thought it was a great gift. Mrs. Trelawney ignored his comment.

"I love it Mr. and Mrs. Trelawney. Thank you so much."

"You're very welcome Lu."

"Glad you like it son." Mr. Trelawney said and I felt warm inside when he called me "son" that made the gift even better.

I passed it over to my mother so she could see.

"Wow. Very nice." She then thanked his parents as well. "Luis loves reading. Always with the books and the writing from when he was a child."

"I didn't know you write as well Lu?" Mrs. Trelawney said.

"Um yea. Just stuff in notebooks. Not really good or anything." I said. I wanted the room to swallow me whole right then.

"Well, remember what the card says." She winked at me and I couldn't help but turn red.

When we finished our cake and coffee, my mother noticed me looking at the kitchen clock. It was already 3pm and I had to be home for 9pm. I was also annoyed with Si about his comment and I hated the feeling because I had never felt like that towards him. He hadn't made me feel small like that in the time we had been together and I didn't like how nauseous I felt.

My mother looked down at her watch. "*¡Ay Dios mío!* Is that the time?"

"Oh yea." Si said. "Would you mind if Lu and I bail too? We have some films we rented and it'd be cool to watch them before he goes home."

"Not a problem son." Mr. Trelawney said.

"Thank you so much Susan and Matthew. Everything tasted beautiful and it was nice to finally meet you." My mother said as she got up.

"Can I give you a ride home Maria?" Mr. Trelawney said.

She waved him off. "No, no. Please. I can take the subway home."

"Honestly, it would be my pleasure and I would feel better."

She looked at me as if she didn't know how to respond. I shrugged my shoulders. Mr. Trelawney was very persuasive. It was another trait I saw in Si.

"Um. Okay but only if you let me help you clear all this up."

"Always a gentleman Matthew." Mrs. Trelawney said.

"More wine mother?"

"I don't find that tone funny Simon."

Si turned to his dad. "Thank you for lunch and for taking Mrs. Morales home." He then looked at his mother. "Always a pleasure."

My mother surprised everyone by stopping Si. "Simon, I know you have better manners."

Si put his head down in shame. He looked as if he wanted to look at me but didn't. Things had gotten weird and now with my mother putting Si in his place, I wanted to be anywhere but there at the moment. She then reached for her purse which was on the side counter, took $10 out of her wallet and handed it to me.

"For a taxi. You don't have much time before you have to be home. Go and enjoy the time together." She then walked up to Si and gave him a hug.

He looked up and smiled at her. His dad watched the whole scene with an expression of tenderness. I wasn't sure why I did it but it felt right to walk over and give his mother a hug. She didn't resist and I took that as a sign that she needed a hug.

As we left, I could hear my mother say "C'mon Susan, some wine helps cleaning."

I felt a chill in the air when we left his parents house. The temperature had dropped a degree or two and it felt like at any moment a leaf could drop off a tree and with it, the end of summer. I walked ahead of Si as we headed towards Amsterdam Avenue to get a taxi.

"Lu. Lu?"

"Would you hold on?"

"Why?" I said as I stopped and turned to face him.

He stopped in front of me and had his hands in his pockets. "I'm sorry baby. I didn't mean for whatever happened in there to happen. She can piss me off sometimes. I just thought for once she might, I don't know, do something that involved my life. Our life?"

"Wait. That was about me?"

He looked at the floor. It had become a bit of a habit that day and it was a side of him I hadn't seen before.

"Do you know how thoughtful their gift was?"

He shook his head.

"After I first met your parents, your mom and I talked about books and she leant me her copy of *Wuthering Heights*. When I returned it, she told me to keep it and consider it a start to building my own library."

"What? Really?" He looked completely ashamed. He walked right up to me and put his arms around me. I put my head against his chest and in that moment, it didn't matter where we were. I needed to feel close to him.

"Don't ever make me feel like that again?" I said.

He kissed me on the head. "I won't. He then sighed. "I guess I owe her an apology."

"Yea. You do." I grabbed his hand. "But you can do that after I leave. Let's go home."

We let our hands go just before the corner. When we got in the taxi, we held hands in the back and the taxi driver although he noticed, didn't say anything. I thought I saw him smirk but it could have been my imagination. By the time we got home, the air had cleared and we decided to watch *Women on the Verge of a Nervous Breakdown*. It was the perfect film to watch after an afternoon with our parents. We started to watch *Indochine* together which was a heavier tone than the Almodóvar film but it was beautiful and I understood why Catherine Denueve was his favorite actress.

The time came for me to get my stuff together and go. Although I knew I would be back to stay on Friday, it felt like an eternity. Si stood by the bedroom door as I started to pack up my things. I stopped and looked at him.

"Why am I taking clothes home?"

He walked over to me and put his arms around me. "Exactly." He kissed me on the lips. "This isn't just my place you know."

I looked at the floor and just under the futon frame was my copy of *A Boy's Own Story* by Edmund White that I was halfway through. I picked it up off the floor and decided everything else could stay.

Si walked me to W4th Street Station so I didn't have to change trains. The sidewalks were quiet but the streets were busy with cars driving by. It seemed like the building lights around us had come on just as we walked on. We hugged and said goodbye just under the awning of The Waverly Movie Theater. Halfway down the stairs I turned around and he was still standing there. We smiled. It was a game we played with one another. I walked a few steps and turned around one last time. He mouthed "I love you, now go."

"I love you too." I mouthed back.

I pulled a token out of my pocket and headed towards the turnstiles. I leant against a pillar as I waited for the D train. I took my Walkman out and pressed play. Duran Duran's "Ordinary World" played through my headphones. It was the right amount of sadness. It felt like Simon LeBon was singing directly to me. I had that familiar feeling of dread as the train pulled into the station.

When I got home, my mother was in her dressing gown and sat at the kitchen table with her word search book.

"Hey Ma."

"*Ay mijo. ¿Porque la cara?* Why the face? You'll see each other again."

"I know."

She got up and hugged me. I stayed for a moment in her embrace before I went to the telephone to call Si and let him know I was home safe.

The last thing he said before we hung up was "Just remember to be yourself."

I sat with my mother at the table and had a hot chocolate. After we left Si's parents house, she had a nice time chatting and helping them clear up the kitchen. She managed to convince his mother to stop by after their dinner and his dad was grateful for that. Mr. Trelawney said to my mother on the drive home that it was his wife's decision making without consulting him that had annoyed him.

When I finished my hot chocolate, I gave her a goodnight kiss.

"*Mijo.*" She said. "They are nice people. That makes me happy."

"Love you Ma."

I stared up at the ceiling fan as I was trying to fall asleep. I thought to myself: *I'm happy. THEY can't take that away from me.*

Seven

"Good luck on your first day, *mijo*." My mother kissed me on the cheek. "I love you."

"I love you too Ma."

I waited for the Bx12 bus to Pelham Bay and thought about how much I wasn't looking forward to the first day of school. I was dressed in blue GAP jeans, a white t-shirt and Si's brown sweater. He had left it at mine and it still smelled of him. I wore it so I could carry him with me on my first day. Underneath my shirt were my Freedom Rings. I couldn't wait to get to Pelham Bay so I could phone him before I got on the next bus. I wanted his voice to be the last one I heard before I got to school.

I had made that journey to Pelham Bay for three years and I had always thought there was something magical how it took me from the urban area that I lived in, past the Bronx Zoo and Botanical Gardens onto the more suburban looking Pelham Parkway. Two very different worlds connected by the bus I rode to school. Then I discovered the Village. After that, the bus ride felt boring.

When I got to Pelham Bay, I saw Rafa at one of the bus stops. He was in a Catholic school uniform and surrounded by guys who had the same dark features he did. He half smiled and then looked away. I knew the drill. Whenever you saw someone from the group outside the Village you ignored one another or if you were able, said hello discreetly. It was our way of protecting ourselves. I thought he would be the ignore type given that he was a fellow Bronxite. It was nice of him to smile. I went to the pay phone and called Si.

"Morning baby." He sounded like he was still in bed.

"Hey."

"I missed you last night." He yawned.

"I missed you too. Weird not sleeping together."

"Do you want me to call you back?"

I gave him the number. The city was trying to get rid of the phones that accepted calls; because of drug dealers but there were still ones that worked. I was happy I had found the one at Pelham Bay. My day was already brighter.

"Any chance you can come down later?" He asked when he rung back.

"Think I need to play it cool with my mom. Oh your parents are coming Friday after dinner. She talked your mother into it."

"How did she do that?" I could hear him making coffee. I pictured him in the kitchen, shirtless in his boxer shirts. His hair hanging to one side as it did in the mornings. I wished I was there.

"Have you ever tried saying no to her."

He laughed. "Yea. True."

"I'll ask her later about this week. But if not, you want to come up?" It sounded so lame when I heard the words out loud. I felt like such a kid.

"Sure." He said.

My pager went off when we were on the phone together. It was Jackie. I said goodbye to Si and phoned her back.

"Hey. What's up?"

"Lu honey, any chance you can come in this week for a few hours?" I could tell by her tone that she had been drinking already.

"Sure but not today or Friday." The perfect excuse to see Si had presented itself. My mother would be okay with me working after school. She was proud of me getting job, even if it was one she didn't quite understand. "I'll call you later and let you know what time tomorrow, ok?"

"Thank you Lu."

I looked at my watch and got on the bus to Middletown Road. The feeling of dread I'd had on the way to school had lifted. I got off at Middletown with a smile on my face and a spring in my step. *Fuck school.* I thought to myself. *You can't bring me down today.*

"Luis? Can we talk?"

My shoulders stiffened and the sound of her voice made me feel sick. Melanie *fucking* Sputano.

I turned around as I summoned every strength in my body to not get angry with her. I was surprised to see she was on her own. I never saw her without her gang of *Guidettes* and rarely without Anthony.

I remained silent and looked at her as if I was channeling Michael Myers from the *Halloween* films.

She looked at me and said "Anthony and I broke up. He's at Rikers now." She then put her hand in the air. "Don't Ask."

I cracked a smile. I couldn't help but think of Mr. Tough Guy Anthony in jail. James always said that the Universe balances itself out. It was the first time I understood what he meant.

"Anyway. Look, you're still gay right?"

"It doesn't wash away." I said.

"Well my cousin Michael told me he's gay and…"

I stopped her. "I have a boyfriend but thanks. I'm flattered." I then started to walk away.

"Luis!! Listen alright! This is hard for me so can you not be such a dick about it."

I stopped and turned back towards her. "What do you want?"

"You still go to that group downtown?"

"Yea. So?"

She looked at me and for the first time I saw a real person looking at me. Not the mean bitch she always was to me.

"Could you maybe. I don't know. Take him with you the next time you go?"

I could see how uncomfortable it was for her to ask but I also had to give her props for trying. It was more than I was capable of showing her and I felt like a bit of a dick for that. I knew Cuchi would be on my side but on my other shoulder I could feel the weight of James and Si telling me to be supportive.

"Sure." I said. "Why don't you come along too?"

"Really?" She then took a step back. "Wait though, I'm not gay."

"No shit." I said "You can still support him."

She looked surprised by what I said and why wouldn't she be? She knew nothing about my world downtown. I knew how small her world was though. We walked towards school and I didn't feel afraid.

When I walked onto the terrace, I expected all eyes on me like that moment in a dream when everyone is staring at you because you're naked.

Nothing happened.

In fact, a few smiled and waved. When Melanie saw her group of friends, she stopped and gave me a kiss on the cheek.

"Thank you Luis." She said before joining her gang. They looked confused by what had just happened.

I was confused. *What had just happened?*

The first day of school had proven to be weird but no one said anything bad or even gave me a nasty look. Maybe with Anthony gone there was room for me to be me? Maybe I could relax a little. After math class I walked downstairs to the pay phones in the cafeteria and bumped into Joey who was in my homeroom. He looked, smiled and continued walking. There was something odd about the encounter. I had known him since freshman year but he kept to himself and didn't speak very often. He was the kind of guy who could make himself invisible at school. I envied him for that. He didn't get picked on like I did. I continued to the pay phones and called my mother to ask her about working for Jackie.

"You better do your homework." She said.

I didn't mention seeing Si but she must've guessed I would as she made it clear that she wanted me home no later than 9pm. I phoned Si later that day before gym class from the payphone outside the Tremont East Diner to tell him that we could see each other the next day and about my day.

"Wow. Melanie *fucking* Sputano?" He said.

"I know. This day has been just been I don't know."

"I'm proud of you though."

"Yea?"

"Yes. I am." He paused. "You amaze me each day Lu."

His words made feel like I was floating high above the city. Knowing that I didn't have to wait till the end of the week made me soar even higher.

When I got off the phone with him, I saw Melanie sitting by herself outside the auditorium smoking a cigarette. She saw me and waved. I waved back and she got up and crossed the street towards me.

"You want to cut last period?" She said.

"On the first day?"

"Yea, fuck it. The day's been long enough."

I shouldn't have said yes but I did. My last period was gym and to be honest, Mr. Jenkins would still be an asshole later that week so I didn't feel I would be missing much by not going.

We went into the diner and sat at a booth away from the front windows so as not to be obvious about cutting class. She ordered a cheeseburger deluxe and a Diet Coke. I ordered fries and gravy and a coke.

Sitting across from her was odd but also nice. I didn't have any friends at school and although everyone was cool towards me on that first day, I also felt on edge about it. Who was to say that Anthony's place wouldn't be taken by someone else?

Melanie talked a lot and I was surprised how funny she could be. It wasn't just how she sounded like someone who was making fun of a Bronx accent but underneath that bitch look I had come to know, she didn't take herself as serious as I thought she did. For the first time, I was laughing with her and not at her or really just hating her.

"You know I call you Melanie *fucking* Sputano, right?"

She laughed. "Oh my Gawd!! That is so funny. You can still call me that if you want."

"But not Slutano."

The waitress came by with our food.

Melanie got serious for a moment. "That one hurt my feelings but I guess I deserved it." She reached over and put her hand on my hand. "I'm sorry for the names I called you."

I took her hand in mine. "Truce?"

She squeezed my hand back. "Truce."

When I got home, I called Cuchi and told her about my day. I told her about Anthony being arrested for stealing a car and cocaine possession.

"Ooooh gurl. That *cabron* is probably somebody's bitch by now."

Even though it was wrong to laugh, we did. I wasn't sad for him though. I was too angry still for the way he treated me. I told Cuchi about Melanie and her cousin coming on Saturday and about seeing Rafa at the bus stop. Cuchi was silent for a bit too long.

"Have you talked to him since Saturday?"

Cuchi sucked her teeth. "He's cute and all but you know

whatever." She then changed the subject. "When we gonna hang out *Papi?*"

"I'm working for Jackie tomorrow and Wednesday after school till about 6.30."

"Let's meet Wednesday. Tiffany's?" Cuchi said. "Get the gang together."

I agreed and then hung the phone up when I heard my mother call me for dinner. The week was shaping up to be a good one and the dread I felt the night before was a million miles away. As I walked away, the phone rang. It was Si.

"Hey. Can I call you back after dinner? We're about to sit down."

"Oh shit." He said. "Tell your mom I'm sorry. Speak later baby."

My mother was humming as she served up the dinner of *chuletas,* white rice and red kidney beans. She never hummed but given the day I had had, nothing else could really surprise me.

"What's with the humming?"

"*Nada mijo.* Just feel good."

I wasn't convinced by her response.

"Okay." I said.

We sat down and I could see that she was distracted and it looked as if she was blushing. I told her about my day and she too was surprised by Melanie.

"*Tu eres bueno.* You know?" She said.

After dinner, I did the dishes. She sat at the kitchen table with a half of glass of wine.

"Do you know I have never been with anyone since your father died?" She said.

"Eww Ma. No. I don't need to be hearing that."

My response made her laugh.

"*Mijo* be serious."

I could tell she was trying to say something and needed help. "Ma. Have you met someone?"

She looked at me as if she had been caught doing something bad. "*Un hombre* asked me out. His name is Guillermo. I know him from the *cuchifritos* near work."

It was the first time I had heard of him or any man she had had an interest in. I couldn't be angry with her over my dad. He had been gone longer than I knew him when he was alive. I could see her embarrassment and the only thing I could think of doing was giving her a hug.

"I'm happy for you Ma." I kissed her on the forehead and went to call Si.

Eight

Jackie was examining some contact sheets against the light box when I entered her loft. The day she interviewed me, I fell in love with the space and would often imagine what it would be like for Si and I to live there together. The old warehouse space had ceilings so high that that it had a level upstairs which overlooked the open plan, that was where Jackie slept and it was the one space she was protective of. I had only ever been up there once when she needed help moving a dresser. The main space had a small kitchen in the corner that more often than not had a collection of half drunken red wine glasses and empty Chinese food boxes. There was a long dining table which was mission control. The walls of the loft were white with exposed brick. Half of the loft was used as her studio and set up with backgrounds, camera stands and photography umbrellas. She had a small sitting area with a Black L shaped couch and an oval lime green coffee table which was often covered in empty coffee cups and an overflowing ashtray. There was no TV in her loft but she did have a stereo and a large collection of music that ranged from Donna Summer to the Indigo Girls to The Rolling Stones and Madonna.

I had never worked anywhere before I met her but as it happened, she had put an ad at The Center looking for a part time assistant. It sounded interesting and meant I could spend more time downtown.

She didn't look away from what she was doing.

"Hi Lu." Her frizzy hair with grey streaks was tied back in a pony tail and she was in her usual black slacks and white shirt with the sleeves rolled up.

"Hey." I walked over to the dining table and there was already a stack of unopened mail to go through. "You know you could probably find an intern that would do this job for free."

"You know how I feel about interns."

I laughed. "Punk ass little know it alls after your contacts?"

"Precisely." She then looked over and smiled at me. "There's some coffee in the kitchen. How's school?"

"Kinda weird." I said and told her about Melanie. About how no one in school seemed to care or remember that I came out at the end of the school year. My mom being asked out, although that had nothing to do with school, just weird.

She took the contact sheet off the light box and then turned towards me. "Lu, none of that is weird. They are good things." She then walked to the coffee table and picked up her cigarettes. "Including your mom getting some action."

"Ewww."

She lit a cigarette and laughed. "You're not the only one allowed to have a boyfriend."

"I guess."

"Look kid. Life is giving you a break. Enjoy it. They'll be plenty of times you are going to wish it did." She took a drag, exhaled and returned to the light box.

I went into the kitchen and poured us both coffees. I hadn't thought of things that way. *Why was it weird that I wasn't be picked on at school? Why was it weird that Anthony was in jail? Wasn't it a good thing that Melanie was being nice to me? Wasn't it a good thing that no one cared that I had a pink triangle button on my backpack?* I had friends who loved me and a boyfriend who loved me and was awesome. So what if my mother might have a….okay maybe I wasn't ready for that one but Jackie was right though, life was good.

I walked over to where she was and handed her a cup of coffee.

"Thanks." I said.

"No worries kid."

I walked away and then stopped, turned around and said, "You're not as scary as you like to make people think you are."

"Mystique darling." She responded in a stronger Queens accent than usual.

I went back to the dining table and started work sorting her mail. I put all her invites to one side. Most were for gallery openings that she attended and stayed for no more than two drinks. I organized her date book and put the contact sheets in project order for the rest of the week. When I left at 6pm to see Si, she was pouring herself a glass of red wine and listening to Velvet Underground.

When I got to Si's, he was on the sofa reading some book in French by Roland Barthes and listening to Ella Fitzgerald singing about April in Paris. He leapt up when he saw me with a grin that reminded me of that cat in *Alice in Wonderland*. He ran over and grabbed me by the waist. We moved to the music as he kissed me on the lips.

"Now the evening is perfect." He said.

Si was more himself since I last saw him. He led me to the sofa and I pushed him down lying on top of him. We were face to face and I could feel us both growing. I looked deep into his brown eyes and he arched his eyebrows. I got up, took his hand and he followed me to the bedroom.

"Are you hungry?" I said as I played with his chest hair.

"I could eat." He pushed my hair to one side with his free hand. His other arm was around me.

"I really want chocolate cake."

"Yea that sounds good. C'mon."

I watched him get up from the futon and put his powder blue boxer shorts on. I thought about what Jackie had said; *sometimes you have to accept that life was good.* He picked up mine and threw them towards me.

"C'mon Lu. I'm not having you miss your curfew."

"Alright."

We finished getting dressed and then headed out of the building towards 7th Avenue South. It was getting dark outside and the streets had a glitter like look when the headlights from the cars shined on them. It made them look magical, like the yellow brick road or something. We turned up towards Caffe Raffiella.

We had been there only once before together and like then, it felt like we had stepped into another world. None of the chairs or tables matched and it was lit by lamps all around the café. The lighting made you feel like you could sit and lose yourself in a book and a cigarette. The waiters were all dressed in shirts and ties which made it feel fancy but not snobby. There were faded murals that looked like somewhere in Italy or Greece. Classical music played in the background at a volume that allowed you to hear and talk. I recognized the piece that was playing as something that Mrs. Trelawney enjoyed listening to when she was reading. It was Bach. I wondered if café's in Europe were all like that.

The short dark skinned waiter with light eyes and what sounded like an Italian accent showed us to a table in the smoking section near the front window. The chairs were oversized with large backs and made me think of the furniture that I had pictured when I read *The Age of Innocence* by Edith Wharton during sophomore year.

The waiter handed us each a menu and then asked if we wanted a drink.

"Viennese coffee." Si said.

"Same please." I remembered that it came in a tall clear glass with whipped cream on top and sprinkled with cinnamon.

"Excellent." He then left us and both Si and I caught each other staring at the waiter's butt which filled out his tight fitting black slacks.

We laughed. He reached over and grabbed my hand which sent an electric shock through my body.

"I'm sorry about that."

"What? Checking out the waiter?"

"Yea." I said embarrassed.

He looked at me in that way he did when he thought I was being silly or in his words, *too cute*. "It's totally normal to notice a good looking guy. I'd think you were lying if you didn't."

"I know but I love what we have and I wouldn't want anything to change that." Since my conversation with Jackie earlier it kept hitting me how great my life was.

He grabbed my other hand. Both of them were now in his. "I love what we have and I couldn't imagine anything changing that." He looked me in the eyes. "I don't want to imagine anything changing that."

I leant in closer to him. "I wish I was staying the night."

"Me too." He gave my hands a soft squeeze.

Our waiter returned with our coffees and Si let go of my hands. It looked as if he had heard part of our conversation by his smile. It was a type of smile I had noticed other people give us when they saw us together. It was like we made them happy by being happy or something. The SAGE guys often gave us the same look.

I ordered a slice of chocolate velvet cake and Si ordered a slice of Black Forest cake. He had a small taste of mine and the way he licked his lips made me hate how little time we had left that night.

As the time drew closer, we talked about school. Si was enjoying his classes as he was able to use his French more. We talked about going to see *True Romance* one day over the weekend as it was opening on my birthday. Moments like that, sat with him down in the Village made my life feel so surreal. My life in The Bronx felt like Luis not

Lu but even people at school started to call me Lu so maybe Luis was fading away and Lu was taking center stage.

We walked as slow as we could to the subway station. We bumped into one another as we exchanged glances and smiles. In a doorway before we got to the subway, we had one long kiss goodnight before we said goodbye.

When I got home, my mother was in a light and happy mood. It was the opposite of what I was feeling.

"*Mijo.* You going to be *con* Simon this weekend?"

"If you let me." I said.

She ignored my comment with her *don't get smart with me* face. "Well *si quiere.* I'm okay with it."

I looked at her like she looked at me when she was trying to figure out what was really going on.

"Why? What do you have planned?" I had become the parent and it was funny to see the look on her face as I questioned her.

"Well if you must be nosy. I'm seeing Guillermo *el Sabado.*"

"Ahh." Then I thought about it more. "Ewww. Yes. I'll be downtown."

"*No me digas* Ewww. You don't think I hear things when Si stays here."

"Ewww Ma. Seriously?!!" I could feel my whole face turn red.

She smiled at having reversed the roles again and left me in the kitchen. I shook my head. What should have been entirely comfortable was for the most part, funny. I called Si. We had all weekend and I would see him, Cuchi and James the next day.

Nine

I was carrying a bag from Li-Lac Chocolates when I met up with everyone at Tiffany's. The chocolates were a birthday gift from Jackie. She joked that her real gift was not coming to my party. I think she would have, had she not already had plans to go to her house in Sag Harbor with someone named Juliette. I tried not to think too much about that.

"Oh gurl. Those are expensive." Cuchi said. She was wearing her signature bob wig and was in better spirits than the last time we saw her.

"Where you been hoeing?" James said.

"Ha…ha..Bitches."

Si kissed me. "Ignore them. They're just jealous *they* can't even get a Kit Kat."

"Then I should be expecting another bag this week, this time from you." I sat down next to him.

"Oooh." Si said and put his arm around me. "I remember when you didn't know what shade was."

"She still don't." James said.

"Mmmhmm." Cuchi added.

Sitting at the diner with my best friends was what I needed the first week of school. It was a huge part of why I was happy. I couldn't wait till Friday for my birthday and the whole weekend with Si but as Jackie said, "enjoy the moment."

After some food, we went to Fat Cats to play some pool and take over their jukebox. The pool hall was empty apart from us so we had freedom to be as loud as we wanted since the staff didn't pay much attention.

As Cuchi shot the eight ball in, she looked at me and winked.

"So *Papi*, you know Rafa right? The one from last Saturday?"

"He called?" I said.

She snapped her finger. "Anyway, I hope you don't mind but I invited him Friday night."

"Sure. Is that okay Si? I turned to Si who was stood next to James and they both had blank expressions on their faces.

I was unsure what had just happened and felt like this was one of those gay learning moments I kept going through like it was a secret handbook you were only given a chapter at a time to read.

"So is he going to meet Cuchi?" James said.

"You can't not bring Cuchi?" Si said. "Cuchi met Lu before Xavy did. It wouldn't be Lu's birthday without her."

Cuchi looked at me and then at James and Si. "*Chicas*. I told him about Cuchi. He's totally fine with it."

James, Si and I looked at each other. I wanted to give the situation the benefit of the doubt. Cuchi wouldn't bring anyone who wasn't cool around us. It wasn't her style and Rafa seemed alright. I walked towards Si and put my arms around him. He softened in my arms and I kissed him on the neck. I could feel him relax. James looked unconvinced.

"Oh I *finally* found a contact for guest list on a Friday night."
James said which lightened the mood.

I screamed and put my arms around him.

"Gurl you ain't getting chocolates from me." He said.

I slapped him on the chest.

Friday night was looking to be the best birthday I had ever had.
There was a party and after my mother left, we would go to
Limelight. Best part was afterwards, we could go back to our own
place. After my Sixteenth birthday dinner, I sat alone in my bedroom
with my copy of *Male Pictorial*, with Ian. I hadn't thought about Ian at
all since I met Si. I didn't need to.

Although I lost every game of pool, it didn't matter. We ended up
at Si's so Cuchi could change into Xavy before heading home and I
could call my mother to tell her I might be running late.

"Just be safe." She said to me. She didn't sound upset and I
wondered if the key to her letting me stay out was her dating or if it
was a test. *What was she up to?*

Xavy and James left together with Cuchi in the bag. I hated that
his parents were the way they were but I also knew that not everyone
was as lucky as Si and I. It's why I never took it for granted even if I
came across as ungrateful at times to my mother.

Si and I lay on the sofa kissing with Belinda Carlisle's "Summer
Rain" playing in the background. As tempted as I was to stay longer,
I had a feeling I needed to get home as close to 9pm as I could. I
made him promise to not eat any of the Li-Lac Chocolates before we

left the apartment so he could walk me to the station.

When I got home, my suspicion that it might be a test was confirmed by her grin and response. "9.15 is not too late."

She kissed me and we sat down together at the kitchen table to chat. I passed.

Ten

My bedroom was cold for early September. The temperature stung my arm when I pulled it out from under the cover to turn on my side and cuddle Si. He shivered against me with the touch of my skin.

My birthday had started out perfect. I kissed his exposed neck and he pressed his body into mine. He titled his head so our eyes could meet.

"Happy Birthday Baby!"

I kissed him on the lips and our bodies moved against one another.

"*Mijos.* You both up?" A knock on the door.

Si and I separated and I fell off the twin bed as a result. I didn't hit my head as one of the pillows we had thrown onto the floor cushioned my fall, it still hurt though.

"Ow. Yea. Ma. *Un momento.*"

Si got up and helped me off the floor.

"To be continued." He said.

"Oh yea."

He winked and put on his jeans and shirt as I searched for my pajama pants and a t-shirt. He kissed me before rubbing his fingers through his hair and then opening my bedroom door. We were hit with the smell of my mother's cooking for the party that night. *Carne guisada, arroz con gandules* and there was definitely some *pernil* going on.

Si's stomach growled.

My mother was pouring coffee when we walked into the kitchen and the radio was on the *noticias*.

"Sleep okay?" She asked Si.

"Yes Mrs. Morales. Thank you for letting me stay over last night."

"Thanks Ma." I blushed as I said it.

She waved it off and motioned us to sit at the table which was laid out with warm bread and butter, orange juice and a box from Twin Donuts which I knew would be full of chocolate frosted donuts with sprinkles. It was a birthday tradition. I hadn't thought about it till that moment that Si and I's first breakfast together was the same, donuts and coffee. *It was meant to be.*

"I have learned that you two always find a way to get together." She waved her hand at us. "At least this way, I know where you are."

Si laughed and gave her a big hug. He used the excuse that he could borrow his dad's car to drive the food down to the Village. My mother thought that was better than her bringing it on the subway.

"*Sientate.* Sit."

She left the kitchen and returned with a gift bag. I opened the card which was one of those cartoon cards that you buy for kids with no recognizable character but it made me smile. I would always be her kid no matter what. The handwriting inside was in Spanish. *Feliz Cumpleaños a mi querido hijo.* There was also a $100 gift certificate for *Tower Records.* I looked at Si who was smiling. There is no way she would have known about that store so I assumed he had told her about it. Most of my music was either recorded off of cassettes I borrowed from the library or from the bootleg guys who used to set up on the Grand Concourse at night.

"Thanks Ma." I said and got up and gave her a hug.

"Don't forget the bag."

I reached into the bag and pulled out a silver wrapped box. I ripped it open and couldn't believe my eyes. "Ma but."

"Ssh. I got a good deal."

"Well c'mon." Si said.

I gave him a look as if he didn't know what it was. I pulled the wrapper off of the box. It was a Sony Discman. I had wanted one for over a year but they were too expensive and we were on a budget. It was a stupid thing to wish for too as my Walkman was fine and it wasn't like I had any CD's to play it with.

I gave her another hug and thanked her. We all sat down and had breakfast together before I had to get ready for school.

When I got out of the shower, Si was lying on the bed listening to *Z Morning Zoo* on Z100 as he looked through the pages of a Sherlock Holmes collection that our old neighbor Mr. Goldstein had leant me before he died. His son had let me keep it and I kept it on the bottom shelf of my nightstand. Like Si's mom, Mr. Goldstein liked to lend me books.

He looked up from the book as I toweled myself dry.

"Want me to drive you to school?"

"I'd love that." I said.

By the time I was dressed and we were ready, my mother had packaged all the food in containers for the party and put them into two separate bags for Si to take with him. Even though the food was sealed, you could still smell it and I had a feeling Roberta would complain about the smell in the hallway. If Si hadn't invited her, I was sure she would invite herself.

My mother kissed us goodbye and we left her to finish getting ready for work.

The only way I knew how to get to school was the way the bus went so we drove that route.

"I never realized how pretty The Bronx is" Si said as we drove past The Bronx River Parkway and onto Pelham Parkway.

With Si by my side, the scenery looked magical again, even more than it did before I discovered going down to Village.

"Does your dad let you borrow the car whenever?" I asked.

"If they're not using it. Why?"

I shrugged my shoulders. "Just wondering."

He smiled as he looked ahead.

"What?" I said. He looked to me as if he was planning something.

"Well. You've never been to my parents house Upstate."

"No we haven't."

He put his right hand over mine and pressed it.

Si parked alongside the Hutchinson River Parkway about half a block from my school so we could kiss goodbye without people seeing us. I knew it was normal for straight teens to experience kissing in a car and it felt awesome. Things began to get a little heavy when Si pulled away.

"Alright Lu, as much as I want to drive away and finish this, your mother would kills us both if you didn't go to school and I have a class to get to."

I sat back against the passenger seat and laughed. "You're right." I said. "You working later?"

"I get off at 4." He said.

"And can we after"

He leant over towards me and kissed me. "Oh yea."

"I love you."

"I love you too baby." He kissed me one more time and looked into my eyes.

I got out of the car and walked the rest of the way to the building. I waved as he drove by. I couldn't wait till later that day when we could finish what we had started that morning.

When I got to the corner, I saw Joey walking from the other direction.

"Waving to your boyfriend?" He said.

"Yup." I said expecting him to say something else.

"Cool." He walked on and I was left wondering what had just happened.

During lunch, I went to the diner on Westchester Square and sat at the very back booth so I could start reading *The Picture of Dorian Gray* by Oscar Wilde. I borrowed it from Si after finishing *A Boy's*

Own Story. Did couples borrow things or were they owned jointly? Although things at school were better than they were it was not like I had any real friends. It could have made the day feel long but Mrs. Trelawney once told me that you were never alone if you were reading. I carried her words with me.

"Hey Lu."

That is you were never alone until you weren't. Melanie *fucking* Sputano.

"Hi" I put my book down.

"Can I join you?"

"Sure."

She sat down and then took an envelope out of her purse and put it on the table.

"It's nothing." She looked away and then back at me. "Don't get excited or anything."

I opened up the envelope and it was a birthday card with a $10 gift certificate for the local bookstore on the square. I smiled and thanked her. Truth is I was touched. She didn't have to do or even say anything but she did.

"Well you know. You're doing me a favor tomorrow and like you're always reading and stuff. Anyway, nobody should spend their birthday on their own."

I looked at her and didn't know what to think after what she said. "Did you follow me here?"

It was her turn to shrug her shoulders. "I saw you with your boyfriend this morning and you looked kind of sad after he left so."

I sat back against the booth and laughed. "Wow. You do have a heart."

"Oh fuck you Luis…I mean Lu." She said and we laughed together.

Having lunch with Melanie *fucking* Sputano was the last thing I expected on my birthday but there we were.

Melanie ordered a cheeseburger deluxe and I ordered a Pizza Burger.

"So are any lesbians going to hit on me?" She said and took a sip of her Diet Coke.

I took a deep breath. "Only if you're lucky."

"Ha ha. Serious though. I don't want to offend but I'm not like that, you know."

One of the things I learned from being with Si and hanging out with BiGLYNY was that sometimes you could get annoyed about things like that. You could make a joke out of it, educate them or do both. It all depended on the mood and the situation. One thing though was that the questions meant, they didn't really get it and you had an opportunity to correct them. Maybe even make it easier for the next gay person they met.

"Well if you hit on me and I said I'm not interested, would you be offended?"

She dipped her French fry in ketchup and thought for a moment. "No, because I know you're gay. Anyway, even if I didn't and I found out you were, I'd get over it."

"There's your answer." I took a bite of my burger.

"So just be polite."

"Pretty much."

"You're easier to talk to than my cousin. I'm glad he's going tomorrow and I think it'll be good for him to meet people but I wish he would talk to me like this." She said as she waved a fry in her hand like it was a wand.

The Melanie *fucking* Sputano who made my life hell during junior year seemed like someone who I don't know, could be a friend? *Maybe?* Senior year would be less lonely with a friend at school. Otherwise, I would spend the day counting down the hours before I could head downtown or finding quiet places to be left alone and read or even wondering what was up with Joey.

I could have told her that maybe he didn't feel comfortable with her. That maybe he needed to find someone he didn't have to explain things to because they knew what he was going through. That perhaps he needed a person who would understand just by one look or one word or sometimes just knowing that he wasn't alone in a room.

"It takes time. He's going through a lot." I said. In the end, it wasn't my place to put words in his mouth.

"Yea, I guess." She ate the fry she was using as a wand.

After lunch, we walked back to the school together and at the gates made plans to meet the following day at The Center for 2pm. I figured it would give them time to be late and time for us to say hello before the meeting started.

"Enjoy the rest of your birthday." She said.

For a moment I thought about inviting her but as we were just getting to know each other, I still found it hard during moments not to remember junior year. *At least I was trying, right?*

After school, I headed towards Westchester Square station and saw near the entrance.

"Going to your boyfriends'?"

I looked around as if it were a set up. "Umm, yea."

"Cool." He then walked on without turning back.

What was with that guy? I thought to myself. *Weirdo.*

I headed into the station and up the stairs to the platform. I was able to get my favorite seat on the subway which was the double seater where I could rest my head against the conductor's booth. I put my headphones on. It was time to zone out. As the train crossed the Bronx River and made its way to Whitlock Avenue before going into the tunnels, I caught myself moving along to Spin Doctor's "Two Princes" as I thought about my only Prince.

Si was waiting outside the bookshop when I got there. He was wearing white wrap around Oakley sunglasses and his hair framed his face around them. We kissed and held hands as we walked down towards home. The best birthday gift I could have asked for was knowing that we were together from then till the end of the weekend.

When we got into the apartment we went right to the bedroom and continued what we had started in his dad's car that morning.

I was lying with my head on his chest as he smoked a cigarette and in that moment, I wanted to cancel the party and just stay in bed with him for the rest of my birthday. Just as I slid my hand down his chest, the intercom rang.

"Ugh. I'll get it."

I didn't bother to put clothes on which caused Si to whistle at me. I pressed the button to speak.

"Hello."

"Ya bitches done fucking."

It was Xavy.

Si and I dressed as quickly as we could. He put some deodorant on and passed it to me. I laughed as I thought how funny it was that we didn't get a chance to shower. He grinned at me as if he had the same thought.

When I opened the door, I was surprised to see Cuchi. I thought Xavy would change at ours before the party. She was wearing a red large wig, black bell bottoms and what looked like my mother's leopard print blouse. Cuchi looked like your favorite *Tía* about to go to a freestyle or salsa club to pick up a guy.

James was behind her dressed in blue jean overalls with one strap down. He had on a white tank top underneath which he would take off when we got to the club. He was the only one of us who had the definition to pull off that look.

"You look fierce *Mami*." I said.

"I know right *Papi*." She handed me a gift bag as did James. "It still sounds weird when you say that word."

I put them on the coffee table and gave them both hugs and kisses.

Cuchi took a bottle of vodka, a bottle of Bacardi and a bottle of coke out of her massive purse.

"Damn girl, got anything else in that bag." Si said as he gave her and then James a hug and kiss.

Cuchi flashed us a devilish grin. "Yes, but that's for later."

The three of them had rum and coke and I had a screwdriver using the leftover OJ in our fridge. Si put on Deee- Lite's *World Clique* album as we got the apartment ready for the party. It was less than two weeks that we had seen them at Wigstock and yet it felt like a different time. I wanted to pinch myself at how different my life had become. Cuchi and James had an extra drink as they danced around but I didn't because I was still scared to be drunk around my mother.

When my mother arrived, the apartment had some banners and candles burning to give the living room a soft touch. Si had put out some small bowls on the coffee table. Some had peanuts, others olives and one had my favorite which were little balls of mozzarella marinated in olive oil, garlic, herbs and some sun dried tomatoes from Zabar's.

Si had made a mix tape for the party and "Erotica" was playing while Cuchi mimed along to it. Had she not screamed with excitement when my mother walked in, it would have been funny to see my mother's face as Cuchi was in stripper mode. She gave everyone hugs and kisses before taking over the kitchen to re-heat the food she had made. Si made sure her wine glass was never empty. He had "borrowed" a few expensive bottles from his parent's wine racks.

Cuchi hung around near the kitchen entrance talking to my mother as she got food in order. James was sat by the window smoking a cigarette and Si and I were snacking from the bowls when the intercom rang.

Eunice and Casey were the next to arrive. Eunice had brought a homemade chocolate cake that had Happy Birthday and my name on it. I introduced her and Casey to my mother. It was a meeting of two mothers. We all thought of Eunice as the maternal leader of the group, a role that was not easy given the range of personalities in BiGLYNY. Casey whispered to me that she thought my mother was hot. My mother must have heard as she smiled and giggled.

Their arrival was a like a domino effect as more members of the group came, along with Roberta who let herself in and was dressed as if she were going to a funeral rather than a party. Her black outfit only needed a veil. She brought with her a tray of Rice Krispies Treats.

"I didn't know what you kids liked to snack on." She said and winked.

"Thank you." I went to kiss her on the cheek and she pulled away.

"Uh uh honey. We're not at that stage yet."

She walked towards the kitchen and I shook my head as I heard her introduce herself to my mother.

Si came up from behind and put his arms around me. I could

smell the Eternity he had put on earlier that day.

"You enjoying yourself?"

I leant back into him and tilted my head up.   "Thank you."

"For what?"

"For all this."

He kissed me on the neck. "Baby, this is all you. All I did was provide the space."

That was hard for me to believe. One of the differences between Si and I was that he had this natural ability to make anyone feel comfortable around him. Everyone seemed to love him from the moment they met him.

As James said about him from the beginning, "He's a good one. He's different."

Me though? I had been without friends most of my life. I was still getting used to people liking me or wanting to be friends with me.

There was a knock on the door and Cuchi answered it. Rafa and Arturo had arrived at the same time. Cuchi hugged Arturo and then stepped right up to Rafa and looked down on him as he tried to figure out what was going on.

"Xavy?" He said.

"Only out of drag *Papi.*" She kissed him on the cheek, leaving an imprint of red lipstick that she then wiped with her finger.

Rafa pinched Cuchi's butt for all of us to see and grinned like a devil. He put his hand in hers and walked towards us to say hello.

Arturo waved in our direction and joined us. "*Ay pero,* the food smells so good."

My mother screamed from the kitchen door which made everyone look in her direction. We all stopped what we were doing as Cyndi Lauper's "I Drove All Night" played in the background. My mother had dropped some rice and beans on the floor but that didn't seem to be what caused the excitement.

"Ma? You okay?" I said as I went to her.

"*¿No puedes ser?* Arturo said.

"*¿Arturo?*" My mother responded in a voice that reminded me of the *telenovelas* she enjoyed watching with a glass of wine or two in the evening.

She put the paper plate of food she was holding on the table and walked towards Arturo. They hugged each other tight and seemed to forget that we were in the room. I looked at Si who shrugged his shoulders. None of us knew what to say or do.

Arturo pulled away and slapped me on the arm. "You never told me your mother was Maria Santiago Cortez?"

"You never asked."

"*Ay* that means, *carajo* shit. When you talked about your *Tío* Jose? He always sounded so familiar."

"*Pero Arturo. ¿Como el puedes saber eso?* That was *otra vida. Otra isla.*"

"What the fuck is going on?"

In unison, Cuchi, Eunice and Arturo said "Don't use that language with your mother!"

I stood back and looked around. Si put his arm around me which helped ground me. My mother motioned with her head to follow her to the kitchen. Casey was cleaning up the spilled food when we walked in. She took one look at our faces and excused herself. My mother was about to speak when she gave Cuchi a look.

"Ma, she's going to know later anyway." I said.

Cuchi and Si both nodded.

Arturo took my mother's hand in his and she smiled at him and took a deep breath.

"Before I met your father, I used to pretend to be Arturo's *novia*. Girlfriend so that nobody would know that he and your uncle were *junto*. Together."

Cuchi gasped and we all looked at her. "*Perdoname.*" She waved her hand to tell us to continue.

"You never told me this before? Why?" I said. I then thought back to what she said at lunch with Si's parents. Guess we weren't the only ones who lied for protection.

She sighed. "I then met your father and well things *se ponieron complicado.*"

Arturo patted my mother on the shoulder. "When they got together. It was hard for Jose and me, to not get found out. Puerto Rico was not that safe for us, so, I wrote to my *Tia* in Chicago and she sent *el dinero* to leave."

"*Y tu Tio.* Well he joined the army so he could get out of Puerto Rico and you know what happened."

I turned towards Arturo. "You never saw each other again?"

"*Una vez* in Chicago before his discharge."

I leant back against the kitchen doorframe. The pieces had fallen into place. That was the reason he was discharged. He must have been caught with Arturo.

"You never spoke again?"

My mother put her arms around Arturo. "No *mi amor*. I wrote but he never answered. When I moved here two years ago, I heard he was sick and…" He trailed off.

"Damn." Cuchi said. "*Aqui como una pendeja.*" She waved air on her face trying not to ruin her makeup as she held back tears.

It cut the tension and made us all laugh. I walked over towards Arturo and my mother and gave them both hugs.

"Even from the grave, he has to be center of attention." I said and smiled at them both. I could see in their faces they needed some privacy so I left them in the kitchen taking Si and Cuchi with me. When we walked back into the party, everyone in the room looked at us.

"Everything's okay. No drama. Just old friends."

"*¡Oye! ¡Respeto!* Arturo said from the kitchen. "Who you calling old?"

Cuchi headed back to Rafa who looked happy to have her back. Eunice and James were by the window smoking. I took Si's hand in mine and walked towards the fire escape window where Roberta was perched. The mix tape was playing "Walking on Broken Glass" by Annie Lennox.

"Your Uncle was a good man." Roberta said. "Another time I'll tell you a story about him." She moved away from the window to let Si and I climb out.

We sat next to each other on the ledge and I put my head against his shoulder.

"What a night?"

"Tell me about it."

"I so want a cigarette now." I said.

"I know baby. Me too."

It was strange that we hid our smoking from our parents. We were both open with them about pretty much everything else. My mother hated cigarettes and although she wasn't wearing her *chancleta* with *Puerto Rico* embossed on them, I was sure she had them in her purse.

Annie finished singing and the music changed to a song that I remember Uncle Jose loved to sing and mime along to when I was a kid and he would look after me. It used to make me laugh because he would put on one of my mother's scarves on his head as if it were long hair he could flip. I looked at Si.

"How did you know about this?" I said.

"I didn't. This wasn't on the tape I made."

We turned around and looked inside the apartment. Everyone was around Cuchi with enough space for her to use the middle as a stage. James pushed me towards the front and Cuchi winked as she started lip syncing to the Peggy Lee classic "Fever" by La Lupe.

"This one's for you *Papi*." She said between lyrics.

My mother and Arturo were shaking along with the music by the entrance to the kitchen and the partygoers smiled and clapped. Cuchi was enjoying every minute and when it came time for the song to switch from English to Spanish complete with salsa dance, she moved towards Rafa who mouthed the words as they danced together. We found out later that his mother was Cuban so he spoke Spanish. As the song finished, she danced over towards me and pulled me into the center with her.

"Happy Birthday *Papi.* ¡*Feliz Cumpleaños!*

I took a bow as everyone clapped and hugged Cuchi.

"I love you." She said and kissed me on the cheek. I could feel the lipstick mark but it didn't matter.

My mother then yelled out "Speech!" This got everyone repeating the word. Rafa put his arm around Cuchi. Casey was giving me that older sister look she was good at. Si and James were smiling right at me.

"Fine." I said and took a deep breath. "Last year was a hard birthday. My Uncle Jose had died and it was just me and my mom. Not that that's bad. She's awesome but you all know that. "I looked over at her and she made a little curtsey. "Truth is, before I met all of you...um, I didn't have any real friends apart from my mom. Wow that sounded lamer than I thought. Sorry Ma." There were giggles in the room. "Thank you for being here. Thank you for being my friends."

James and Eunice started singing the theme from *The Golden Girls* and everyone else joined in. Si walked over to me and gave me a kiss.

"Oh get a room."

We turned to see Mr. and Mrs. Trelawney who had just arrived. Mr. Trelawney's cheeks had a tinge of red which he got when he drank a few glasses of wine. Mrs. Trelawney was smiling as if she had had a good night already. They greeted us with big hugs. I noticed when Si hugged his mother there was none of the tension from Sunday. The night felt complete with them there. I saw Si look at my mother and she bowed her head in a "you're welcome" manner.

James dimmed the lights and Eunice came out of the kitchen holding the lit birthday cake. Everyone started to sing *Happy Birthday*.

After cake, Si's mix tape took a more upbeat dance tone to prepare us for going out after everyone left. My mother and Arturo decided to go on somewhere else together to continue catching up. I wasn't convinced that was a good idea but I guess I had to trust her. Mr. and Mrs. Trelawney stayed for a bit longer. It was fun watching her move her hips to "Rhythm is a Dancer." Before they left, Mr. Trelawney left us a VHS copy of some new show called *The X-Files* that he said we had to see. Soon after, the party emptied out and it was just the four of us.

Si and I shared that long awaited cigarette and James rolled a joint while Cuchi decided if she was going out or Xavy was.

Eleven

I rolled off the futon and onto the floor which was not the way I had wanted to wake up after my birthday. I looked at the alarm clock and it was still early but Si wasn't in bed. I sat up and put my boxer shorts on, a t-shirt and went out to find where he might be.

I opened the bedroom door and saw Xavy undressed but Cuchi's face still on. She was on the floor covered in a blanket and I got the feeling she was not going to enjoy taking her makeup off when she woke up. James was on the sofa with a smile on his face as he slept. I could hear Si in the kitchen filling up the coffee machine.

I walked in and put my arms around him from behind. He leaned back against me.

"Well good morning to you."

I pressed my head against his back. "Thank you."

He turned the machine on and then turned around so we were facing each other. He looked down into my eyes.

"You're welcome baby."

It was a peaceful start to the morning. I didn't remember staying long at Limelight but I remember dancing from room to room. I vaguely remembered the tracks "Dancing Queen," "Push the Feeling On" and I think the *Speed Racer* theme. It was all one track after another in my head.

The smell of freshly ground hazelnut coffee was filling the kitchen and I couldn't wait for my first cup of coffee. There was a scream from the living room which made us both jump.

"Fuck you!" We heard Xavy say.

Si and I went to the kitchen doorway and saw James smiling as he pointed to Cuchi. Her eyeliner made her looked like a rabid raccoon and there were remnants of glitter on her wig. She got up, flipped us all her middle finger and went into the bathroom with her bag.

"Thanks for letting me stay." James said.

"Anytime." Si said.

Xavy came out of the bathroom wrapped in a towel as we sat around with cups of coffee and cigarettes listening to Toni Braxton which James had put on. He couldn't take anymore high energy music that early. Xavy walked into the kitchen and came back with a cup of coffee and sat down.

"Gurl! What happened last night?" He rubbed his temples.

"Well I had to drag your ass out of the darkroom." James said.

Si and I looked at Xavy surprised.

"Nice choices of words bitch."

James laughed. "Nothing but dancing *Mami*. For once."

We had more coffee as we took turns getting showered and ready to head to Tiffany's for breakfast. I called my mother who was still in bed. Arturo and her ended up at Escuelita. *My mother at a gay club? Even I hadn't been there.*

"Have fun tonight on your date Ma." I said.

"*Carajo*. Shit. I have to get some more sleep. I love you *mijo*." She hung up.

The day had a hint of summer about it as we walked up from Tiffany's after breakfast to The Center. Part of it was the weather but most of it was that we spent as much of the summer together and it felt like a continuation of my birthday. There was no doubt we would end up on the piers after the meeting although had it not been for BiGLYNY, I would have preferred to walk the city with just Si. We started to do that more towards the end of the summer and there was so much of the city to see. I loved the Village but New York was full of doors waiting to be opened and I was ready to kick them down.

When we turned the corner onto 13th Street, Rafa was waiting in front of The Center. He saw us walking towards him and walked towards us. He met us halfway with a single rose in his hand.

"What's this?"

"Well, I was going to give it to Cuchi but I guess Xavy will have to have it."

Xavy blushed.

Rafa handed it to Xavy and gave him a kiss on the cheek.

James turned to us. "Something about that one."

"They're happy." I said.

We walked on and sat on the stoop in front of The Center and waited for Melanie and Michael to arrive. We weren't sat long when I recognized her walking towards us. Well, I recognized her hair which was bigger than usual. She was dressed in a tight skirt, heels and reminded me of one of those Staten Island girls in that film *Working Girl.*

"Bridge and Tunnel alert." James said.

I slapped him on the arm as I laughed.

Si got up. "If that's Michael, today should be interesting."

"What? Hold up!" James said. "Oh damn!"

I had been caught up in how ridiculous Melanie looked that I didn't notice Michael who was walking next to her. He was gorgeous. There was no doubt about that. He had skin the color of Ralph Macchio but his hair was a light brown, almost dirty blonde and he his eyes were a deep blue. He was tall and walked as if he owned the street. He was dressed in khakis, suede Bass shoes and a blue button down Ralph Lauren shirt. Over it, he had a black leather jacket and a backpack. If he was nervous, he didn't show it.

"Damn! *Papi.* Shorty need a ride?" Xavy said out loud which made Rafa slap him on his arm.

"What?" Xavy winked at Rafa and blushed.

"Hi Luis." Melanie said. "I mean Lu."

"Hi."

All eyes were on Michael, who looked as if he was enjoying the attention but also nervous.

I introduced Mel to everyone. James couldn't help adding, "Oh I remember you."

"Can I just say that I'm sorry for that."

James responded with a side eye.

Michael introduced himself as Mel was caught up in feeling out of place and weird because of James' comment. You could tell in his soft but firm tone that he was not from the city. He also looked you in the eye when he said hello. He was the opposite of Melanie *fucking*

Sputano and apart from the same last name; they couldn't have looked, sounded or been more different. He opened his backpack, pulled out an envelope and with it a copy of *Their Eyes Were Watching God* by Zora Neale Hurston fell out on the sidewalk. James bent down and picked it up.

"School assignment?"

"I love African American writers." Michael said.

James handed it back to him. "Is that all you love about African Americans?"

Michael blushed and handed me the card. "I hope you don't think it's weird but Mel mentioned it was your birthday and well here, as a thank you for today."

"Gurl, I love me a well mannered man." James said to Xavy.

"Since when you like them White?"

James stood tall. "I don't discriminate." He then smiled at Michael.

"Thank you." I said to Michael. "You didn't have to."

We chatted while we waited for the rest of the group to arrive and make our way into the meeting. Michael was a senior at Fordham Prep which was not too far from where I lived. He lived in Briarcliff Manor, which was another world from the city even though it was close by. I watched as James hung on his words. Each time he giggled, Michael would blush and I could see he was trying his best not to focus on James. He failed though.

In the meeting, James sat on one side of Michael, Melanie on the other side. She was between me and Michael. When Michael introduced himself, the group responded with a flirtatious sounding,

"Hi Michael."

Then Melanie introduced herself.

"Hi. I'm Mel. I'm not a lesbian though. I'm here to support Michael, my cousin here." She said as she pointed to him. He put his arm around her.

"Welcome." Eunice said.

It was my turn to speak but Mel cut me off.

"Sorry, can I just say something else?"

"Of course." Eunice said.

"I go to school with Luis here. Sorry I mean Lu." She pointed at me. "I've not always been accepting of you guys and I'm embarrassed by that. Thank you for accepting me here and to Lu for making me realize that there's nothing wrong with you guys."

Casey started to clap and she had a smile on her face. Eunice joined in as did the rest of the group. Si nudged me to join them which I did but I wasn't happy about it.

"Mel, can we talk more about that during the session?"

Mel nodded and sat back in the chair. It was my turn to speak and I didn't know what to say. I was pissed off that everyone thought she was sweet and that her saying she learned was enough. We had had some nice conversations since school started but was that enough? I needed her to know that it wasn't enough for me and that if she was going to be there for Michael, she needed to know how crucial it was that she learned. Not just say the words.

Si grabbed my hand and I sat up.

"Why did you have such a problem with us? With me? Why did

you just stand there and let Anthony beat me up?" I couldn't stop. "Why did *you* start the fight sometimes?"

The group was looking in our direction.

"Lu, lower your voice. You know the structure of the group." Eunice said. Her tone had become stern, a reminder that she was an Advisor.

"Let her answer." Rafa said to my surprise.

"C'mon Eunice. How often do we get a chance to confront our attackers?" Si said as he held my hand tight.

Mel looked as if she wanted to sink into the floor. I began to tremble and Si put an arm around me.

She held her hand up. "It's okay." She turned her body towards me. "My dad doesn't like gays. He doesn't like most people who aren't Italian or white. He can just about deal with Hispanics."

Michael nodded his head. His arm was still around her to steady her.

Mel continued. "I grew up hearing all bad stuff about everybody. My mom thinks the gays are funny like her hairdresser or anyone who's flamboyant in a store or something." She then looked around. "I didn't know better." She turned back to me. "Anthony was a dick and it was easier to go along with him than fight him. Believe me."

"I can deal with being called a fag. I can even deal with the punches. What I can't deal with is people standing by and letting it happen. That's what hurt the most." I looked at Michael and then at her. "Promise me you'll never be one of those people. Promise Michael you'll never be one of those people."

Mel took my hand and Si let go of me. Michael loosened his arm around her. Both of our eyes were red. The room around us was silent. "Lu, I promise you, everyone here and especially Michael that I will never stand by and not say anything the next time someone says something homophobic." She took my hand in hers. "I promise."

"Thank you." I got up from the chair and pulled her up and gave her a big hug.

The room clapped around us and Michael got up and hugged Mel too. I looked at Eunice who was clapping the loudest and she gave me a look like she was proud of me.

"Right." She said. "I think this is the perfect time to move onto something lighter, like wishing Lu a Happy Birthday." The room started singing and Casey brought out a cake similar to the one Eunice had brought to my party the day before. The mood in the room changed completely and some of the group went up to Mel and Michael to chat.

I excused myself from Si and walked outside to the courtyard for some air and one of the guys from SAGE was sat in the sun, smoking a cigarette.

"You kids are so much braver than I ever was." He said.

"I don't know. I think we're just as scared."

He ashed his cigarette. "I heard through the door what was being said." He sighed. "If I had had the courage you did to confront your attacker? Well…" His voice trailed off and he took a drag.

I didn't know what to say. I didn't think there was much else to say so I walked over and gave him a hug. It seemed like the right thing to do.

"Thank you." He said.

"Thank YOU."

I turned around and Si was waiting by the entrance to the room the meeting was in. He held out his hand to me and when I put my hand in his, he pulled me towards him.

He was looking right into my eyes. "I'm so proud of you. What you did in there took guts."

I wrapped my arms around his waist and put my head against his chest. "I couldn't have done that without you."

"Lu, you can do anything."

I stopped him and looked up at him. "Si, you and me. This. This is why I feel strong enough to fight and not take shit."

He pushed some of my hair to one side. "Baby, you've always had that strength. You are strong, with or without me."

The way he looked at me made me believe him.

"Right bitches! Pier time!" Xavy said as he entered the courtyard.

I looked at my watch. "It's early though."

"Yea well Eunice and the Council decided after your *Ricky Lake* moment, it was better for all of us to go down to the piers and hang out."

"Wait, the whole group?" Si said.

"Mhmmm, so let's go cause I aint' walking with the amoeba." Xavy said. He often referred to the group as a whole as a dysfunctional amoeba when it came to doing anything outside The

Center.

Xavy and Rafa walked alongside us and in front were Mel, Michael and James. The spark between Michael and James made me happy. Casey caught up with us and we headed down to the Piers.

The Piers weren't as busy as they had been during the summer but once the entire group was there, it turned into a carnival. We sat in our usual place beyond the fence on the edge. Even Melanie *fucking* Sputano didn't look out of place anymore. Life was strange. The last time I had seen her in The Village, she was with that prick Anthony and Cuchi had put him in his place. There she was with her gay cousin hanging out with us.

She saw me look at her and got up from where she was sitting with Michael and James. She pulled me to one side.

"Thanks for giving me another chance. For giving me a chance."

We both looked over in the direction of Michael and James who had moved closer and were in a world of their own.

"Somehow I think my Uncle would be okay with him being gay, but gay AND a black boyfriend."

I put my arm around her. "And that's where you come in."

She leant against me. "He was always so quiet and shy but look at him." She said. "He looks happy."

"It's because he's being himself. It's why we come down here. It's why we meet once a week at least. It's the one day of the week that we can be ourselves."

"That's sad." She put her head against me shoulder."

"It's better than not having any day."

Si came over and put his arms around both of us. "Right you two! No more serious talks." He pulled a joint out of his cigarette pack and handed it to me. "Go birthday boy."

I handed it to Mel. "Ladies first."

She lit it up and took a drag. She then passed it to me and soon we were joined by Xavy, Rafa, Michael and James.

We sat at the very edge of the pier passing it between us as The Circle Line floated by. We must have looked like the pier version of that picture of Old New York with the guys on the suspended bar of steel having their lunch high above the city streets.

Twelve

The sky was grey when I woke up to make coffee. As it brewed, I went back to bed and crawled under the blanket without disturbing Si. He was a deep sleeper and he had this peaceful look about him. I watched him for a few minutes. I was happy that we hadn't stayed out late with the gang. Sunday was our last day of the weekend together and it was nice for it to be just us.

He opened one eye. "Yes?"

"Just happy that it's you and I." I said. "Alone."

He put one arm around me and pulled me under. "Me too baby."

"What do you want to do today?" I said as I snuggled into him.

"Whatever you want to do. It's still your birthday weekend."

"Oh yea. It is." I had never had such a big deal made about my birthday and I liked it.

Si first took me to Tower Records on Lafayette about a month after we had gotten together. We had been walking around the East Village and stopped for lunch at 7A. They were playing The Cramps' *Flaming Lips* and as soon as we left, he had to go and buy it. I had never been in a record store like it before. It seemed to carry anything you could think of and more. Si was looking at imports from Europe as I walked around unsure of where to begin.

I had a new CD player and money to spend which meant that of course, I wanted everything. Si had a lot of CD's so I knew I could borrow those whenever I wanted. *What would I want though?*

Hmm. There was Belinda Carlisle's "Greatest Hits," but Si had all her albums. Pet Shop Boys? I did love "Domino Dancing." What about REM? "Losing My Religion" was a great song. So was "Radio Free Europe." Maybe I should look at Techno CD's. I did love to dance.

I looked over where Si was and saw him talking to some guy. The guy was similar build to Si and had on an NYU sweater. He looked like he belonged in one of those 80's films where the preppy guys were assholes. There was no doubt the guy was into Si by the way he pushed his black hair back and smiled as Si spoke. He would have been cute if he wasn't hitting on my boyfriend. *Who the hell did this guy think he was?* I started to feel like some deranged jealous wife from a soap opera. I took a deep breath and walked towards where they were but bumped into one of those spinning racks which I tried to catch from falling but I just looked as if I was dancing with it. It was at that moment that the guy saw me and then Si turned around.

He ran towards me and held the rack so I could get off it. "You okay?"

I wasn't okay. I had made a complete ass of myself. "Yea I'm fine." He came around and put his arm around my shoulder. The guy walked over towards us.

"Lu. This is Jamie." *Of course he is.* I extended my hand.

"Hey." Jamie said and turned his attention back to Si. "So maybe see you later?"

"Maybe."

Excuse me! I thought although what I said was "What's later?"

Jamie walked away after shaking his head in that polite way that I hated because it felt like I wasn't someone interesting enough to even say good bye to.

"Later." Si said and turned to face me.

"What's later?"

Si looked at me and it felt like he hadn't really understood what had just happened. If Cuchi had been there, she would have read the moment to filth.

"Some of the guys in my program are performing *chansons* at the French Roast on 6th Avenue."

"Oh."

Si smiled as he looked at me. "Are you jealous?"

I shook my head. "Who's Jamie?" His name came out of my mouth as if I had tasted something bad.

"We have French Lit together."

I tilted my head like the girls on my block when they didn't believe what they were being told. I hated myself for it too. Here we were having a moment like that when I had to go home that night. It didn't matter if he went out or not because I knew I would be home staring at the ceiling fan and thinking all sorts of crazy things.

He touched my shoulder as I looked the other way.

"Hey. Lu. Look at me."

I couldn't though. I had this feeling in my stomach, it was heavy and uncomfortable. I was no longer in the mood to shop for CD's. I went to walk away but he stopped me.

"Lu. Let's talk."

He grabbed my left hand and his fingers tickled the palm of it. We left Tower Records and walked down Lafayette. We walked past Colonnade Row. They were my favorite buildings around that area because although they were preserved from another time, the extensions made them look like they were playing dress up and getting it slightly wrong. I wanted to go back in time to when Si first showed me them. I wanted to go back before Jamie and Tower Records. I had no idea where we were heading.

"Si! Stop! This is so stupid! Where are we going?"

He stepped in front of me. He wasn't angry though. He wasn't even annoyed. He smirked and it was odd but it helped clear some of the tension between us.

"Where it all fell into place."

"Oscar Wilde?" It didn't make any sense to me and we were walking a very convoluted way back to the West Village if that was what he meant.

He grabbed my hand. "Trust me."

We walked on till we got to The Angelika. We had been there a lot over the summer but I still had no idea what he meant about all of it falling into place. We went inside and took a seat by the window. Si ordered two coffees. He sat across from me smiling and his knee pressed against mine.

"Do you remember the first time we came here?"

"Our first real date?"

He nodded his head and smiled. "It was raining and my parents were having people over to the house so we couldn't go back there."

The date came back to me. We met up for lunch at Dojo's near Washington Square Park and afterwards we watched *The Trial*. It wasn't the most romantic choice but we were able to hold hands in the movie theater and that made the choice perfect.

"We couldn't even go back to The Bronx because my mom had just met you and I wasn't ready to ask her if you could come over." I said.

He giggled and pressed his knee harder against mine. "Yes and after the film, it was still raining so we had a coffee here, at this very table."

"Then after it stopped." I said. "We walked up 6th Avenue doing that bumping against each other thing that we do."

"Secret kissing." He said and put his hand over mine.

"Do you remember where we stopped on the way?"

I thought for a moment. I remember we walked pretty much the same way we had that first night together after Limelight. That afternoon though we entered Central Park by the statue of Simón Bolívar. We walked past The Dairy and over Sheep Meadow in the direction of Strawberry Fields and then alongside The Lake. It was humid because of the on/ off rain that day and the grey skies made me wish we could spend the day indoors under a blanket in an air conditioned room. It started to rain as we walked past one of the pavilions on The Lake and we ducked into it.

"Yea, we took cover from the rain."

"That's right. It was just us and I kissed you right there on the lake for what felt like forever."

The feeling of that kiss came back to me because I remembered how magical it was. The rain was beating down on the wooden roof above us and my legs got wet from the raindrops falling into The Lake and splashing onto the pavilion floor. It was like we were the only ones in Central Park.

Si looked down at his coffee. He took a sip and then looked up at me. "I knew that moment for sure that there would never be anyone else. That all I wanted was you." He took another sip of his coffee and cleared his throat. "Lu, that was the moment I fell head over in heels in love with you and each day is better than the day before."

I squeezed his hand. My stomach fluttered. I couldn't help but smile, and sort of giggle but it wasn't a giggle, it was like I couldn't believe how beautiful that moment was and it made me want to cry but only because I was happy.

"I'm sorry for being an idiot." I said. "From the moment I saw you, I knew I wanted to be with you and I guess I get scared that you'll, I don't know."

"Hey, not a chance." He caressed my hand and smiled. "We can't control if someone finds us attractive but you and me, we can remember this conversation, whenever we feel insecure."

"We?" I said.

"Yes, we." He leant back in his chair. "I get scared too."

I looked at the clock in the lobby. I knew we would have to say goodbye that evening and all I wanted at that moment was to be alone with him.

"Can we go home?" I said.

"You read my mind."

We spent the rest of that day in bed under the forest green blankets he had bought at Bed, Bath and Beyond. We ordered pizza and listened to Enigma and The The. As we were dressing, he asked me if I minded him going out to see his classmates sing.

"Have fun." I kissed him on the lips and he put his arms around my waist.

"I'll page you when I get home. Maybe we can chat?"

"I'd like that."

He held me tight for a bit longer and then pulled away.

"Right. Anymore of that and you won't make it home tonight."

I walked him to French Roast and we kissed in front of the entrance. I saw Jamie sitting in the window and he looked away like he was jealous. I wasn't though. We said goodbye and I crossed the street. When I turned around, Si was still there with his hands in his pockets. He took one out, waved at me and blew me a kiss.

I mouthed "I love you."

"You too." He mouthed back and winked. I turned around and continued walking towards the subway.

I could trust him. It was stupid of me to think I couldn't.

When I got home, my mother was getting her stuff ready for the week. I dropped my bag in my room and sat with her in the kitchen as she ironed.

"How was your date?"

"Ay *Mijo*. He was a gentleman."

"Where'd you go?"

"*El Chino*. I just thought you know in case *el era raro*, you know weird then at least Hector was there."

That made me happy. All my life she was cautious and it protected us. It is why she hated not knowing where I was or lies. Knowing was better than not knowing.

"So you seeing him again?"

"*Sí claro*. I want you to meet him. *¿Este Viernes?*

'Sure. I guess he needs the man of the house's approval?"

She smirked and nodded her head.

"I'll tell Si."

She put the iron down and looked at me. "*Mijo*, you know Simon is like a son to me and I support you but maybe not this time?"

I looked at her in disbelief.

I hadn't expected that response. How open had I been with her? How open did she demand me to be with her? I felt like I was being pushed into a closet. Did she even tell him that I was gay? Did I even come up? I thought it would have been important for her to be honest about things.

"Wow." I got up and walked out of the kitchen.

She went to grab me but I shrugged her off. She followed me to my room. "*Mijo* wait."

I didn't know what to do but I knew I had to get out of there. I had to get away from her hypocrisy, her double standards. I picked my bag up.

"*¿Adonde vas?*"

I went to walk past her. "Where do you think?"

"We had a deal. *Un trato.* Not on a school night."

I looked at her and I could see how upset she was but I didn't care. She had no right to guilt trip me.

"Yea well, I thought you valued honesty."

I left the apartment and headed to the subway. I tried to hold back my tears as I rested my head against the window of the D train back to West 4th Street.

I was sat on the sofa with just a lamp on when Si got home. I had shut my pager off because I got tired of hearing it buzz. It didn't take a genius to figure out who it was.

"Lu? What's up?"

I ran towards him and lost it. He held me as I went limp in his arms. He guided me back to the sofa and took my hand in his as I told him what had happened. He rubbed the palm of my hand as I spoke and reassured me with each stroke.

"Hey. Let me make a phone call."

"Are you calling *her?*"

He didn't need to answer.

I got up and walked into the bedroom. I could hear him on the phone.

"He's upset but he's safe…It'll be fine… I promise he'll make it to school tomorrow… Okay, Mrs. Morales….you too."

I was under the blanket on the futon when he came in. He looked down at me with the sweetest smile.

"How was the music?"

He giggled. "It was good. I think you would have liked it."

How was *Jamie?*" I said.

He joined me on the bed and laughed. "I think we made *our* point clear when he saw us say goodnight."

"Was it that obvious?"

He put his head on my chest and his arm across me.

"Hope you don't mind me being here." I said.

He lifted his head and looked at me. "Are you kidding? This was the best part of my night."

"Was she mad?"

"She's hurt. Get some sleep and talk it out with her tomorrow."

"It doesn't seem to bother you." I said.

He patted my chest. "She's still learning to be the mother of a gay son and you're still learning that the world isn't always fair to us. You'll sort it out. Trust me. She's a good mother."

Thirteen

In that moment between squeezing him and opening my eyes, I had forgotten about the night before but that feeling didn't last long. The argument with my mother came back twofold.

We walked towards Washington Mews together and I left Si outside the gates.

"Call me later." He kissed me on the forehead.

"I will."

"Don't be so hard on her Lu."

"I promise."

We walked away and then both turned at the same time. His look made me melt. I knew he was right about her. I just didn't know how we would talk or what I would say. I bumped into Jamie as I turned onto 8th Street.

"Oh sorry." He said and then it clicked who I was. "You're Si's boy."

"And you're not." I smiled and walked on.

I took the 6 train from Astor Place. I listened to Depeche Mode's "Shake the Disease" on repeat on the ride up to school.

I got off the train at Westchester Square and walked up to the school building from there. I saw my mother's maroon Toyota Celica parked near the football field just before the entrance to the terrace. I tapped on the window and she lowered it.

"Want to talk?"

She unlocked the door. I got in and we headed towards Pelham Bay.

"I'm sorry…" I started to say but she cut me off.

"*No Mijo*, I'm sorry." She parked the car near the station and we walked to the deli and grabbed a couple of ham, egg and cheese sandwiches with coffee to go. We then walked into the park and sat down on a bench near the War Memorial.

"I don't know how people drink this *meirda*."

I laughed.

"Ma…"

She raised her hand. "I raised you right *y tienes razón*." She was looking forward and I could tell that it was hard for her to admit that. "*Mijo*, I love you for who you are. I love Simon *tambien. El eres bueno para ti.* You two are good together. I don't worry about you when you are with him."

"I never thought how hard all of this must be."

She shook her head. "*Mijo*, no. Never apologize for who you are. It's not hard. It shouldn't be hard. I was scared that Guillermo might not still like me if I had a gay son. *Cuando fuiste,* I walked around the apartment and it was so empty. I felt so alone *pero* I can handle being alone. What I can't handle is not having my son. I was so scared I lost you." She put her sandwich and coffee next to her on the bench and wiped her face.

I hadn't thought about that. About how she might feel alone when I wasn't home. It had been the two of us since Uncle Jose died and all I wanted to do since I came out was spend it with Si or with friends. I didn't realize how much the distance hurt her.

I put my arm around her.

"I'm sorry for not being home as much."

She looked at me and smiled. "I called Guillermo and told him that I have a gay son and that I wanted him to meet you and Si on Friday."

"Really?"

"*Sí*"

I hadn't expected that. "What did he say?"

She smiled even more. "That he couldn't wait. That he hopes one day I could meet his daughter who lives in Chicago. She's a lesbian."

We both started laughing at the same time. It wasn't that his daughter was a lesbian. Just the whole situation. James would have said "the universe has a plan for us all *Papi*."

"Are we going to be okay Ma?"

"*Mijo, claro*. This is new for both of us."

"That's what Si said."

"I told you he was good for you."

He was more than just good for me. He was perfect. "*El Chino*, again?"

She grinned. "It's close to the subway. You can then go to that club you don't think I know you go to."

Months ago I would have tried to downplay her comment but all I could do was laugh. Things were different now and we had just moved up a level in our relationship. I shrugged and didn't contradict her comment.

We finished our sandwiches, coffee and walked back to the car. She drove me back to school. The bell had run already as there was no one on the terrace. Before I got out of the car she tapped me on the arm.

"If you want to see Simon from now on whenever, it's ok. Just don't forget *que tienes una casa.*"

I kissed her on the cheek. "I love you Ma."

"You too *mijo.*"

Before heading to math class, I went to the cafeteria and used the pay phone to leave a voicemail for Si.

On my way home, I saw Rafa at the bus stop with some school friends as I was waiting for the Bx12. He winked at me as an acknowledgement. It was progress. I found it funny how people didn't realize the subtle way we communicated out in the open. Then it pissed me off that we had to be subtle at all.

Joey walked past me and whistled. It was creepy and I couldn't figure out what his deal was. I didn't feel threatened by him but I also never saw him with anyone so I was a bit nervous around him.

When I got home, my mother was at the table having coffee with a man. He got up and looked a bit ashamed.

"*Mijo,* I thought you would be downtown."

"I thought about it but after this morning, I thought it would be a nice to have the night together."

"Oh did you?" She said.

The man introduced himself. "I'm Guillermo." He extended his hand.

"*Mucho gusto.*" I shook his hand. He had a firm grip and I tried not to wince.

"Don't let me disturb you." I said. "I need to use the phone." I walked past them and saw how embarrassed my mother looked. It was funny. Also, I was impressed. Guillermo was better looking than I thought. He looked like he took care of himself. He had salt and pepper hair with dark eyebrows, hazel eyes, olive skin, and a nice smile to match.

I called Si back and told him about the talk with my mother and about Friday. He was relieved and we made plans to spend the next night together.

I watched my mother see Guillermo out. He gave her a peck on the cheek. It was nice to see her blush. I couldn't remember a time that she had shown an interest in any man. I guess with looking after me and Uncle Jose, there wasn't that much time left for her.

Uncle Jose used to tease her with his crude sayings. "*Si no la usas, la pierde.*" Not the kind of thing you wanted to hear about your mom's privates. That was Uncle Jose though, he loved to shock.

She closed the door and leant against it with her eyes closed. She had her hand on her chest like a teenager. She opened her eyes and saw me smiling back at her. She blushed.

"He's cute, Ma."

She opened her eyes wide. "I know! Right?? *¡Guapisimo!*"

"Si is looking forward to Friday."

"Me too. You going to see him later?"

I shook my head.

"*¿Todo esta bien?* Everything okay?"

"Of course. I just thought tonight that we could hang out."

She walked over to me and gave me a big hug. "I would love that."

"I'm going to see him tomorrow night okay?"

"*Claro Mijo.*" She kissed me on the cheek.

Fourteen

Hector Chan was smiling from ear to ear when he saw the four of us walk in for dinner.

"*¡Maria! Mi amorsita. ¡Luis!*" He gave us both big hugs. He shook Guillermo's hand and he surprised Si by giving him a hug and two kisses in the French style.

"*Ça va Simon?*" He said in the clearest sounding French accent.

"*Ça va bien Monsieur Chan merci. Ça va?*" Si said. I only ever heard him speak French with his mother. It was usually when they didn't want anyone to know what they were saying. She had made sure he learned French as a child in Paris and he attended bilingual schools in both London and New York. We both knew what it was like to live between two worlds and it was something that we bonded on. He sounded sexier speaking French than I did speaking Spanish. *Maybe it was because I associated Spanish with my mother?*

"*Très bien, merci.*" Hector had never been to France but he learned French at school. According to my mother, he was just one of those people who could pick up any language he wanted to and become fluent in it. He also remembered little things about everyone he met which made him a great host. He showed us to our booth and took our drinks order.

"So you speak French, Simon?" Guillermo asked.

"*Oui.* I'm majoring in French at NYU."

"And he was born in Paris." I said. Si looked at me as if that was unimportant. I don't know why it sounded more exotic to me than being born in New York.

"I went to Paris once on leave when I was stationed at Ramstein in West Germany. Beautiful city. It was like a living museum." Guillermo said.

I looked at my mother who was admiring Guillermo as he spoke. It felt like we were on a double date. *Was it a double date?* Was I trying to figure out if Guillermo was good for her? *Both?*

"It is. My mum would go back in a heartbeat. My dad would love to go back to Cornwall. That's where he's from." He said. "So we live in New York."

Guillermo laughed. "A compromise."

"You mother, she doesn't like New York, *no?*" My mother said.

Si thought about it for a moment. "I never thought about it like that. I think she was happy in Paris because they were younger."

Guillermo looked at my mother and then the two of us. "Happiness is something you can only appreciate with age."

Hector returned with a piña colada for my mother, a beer for Guillermo and two cokes for us. He also put a pot of tea on the table and then two small glasses of red wine for Si and me. He looked at my mother.

"Un probito para la cena. Como en Francia."

She approved with a smile and he left the table.

Guillermo went to make a toast but stopped when he looked at me and then bowed his head a little. The whole macho head of the house thing was so not me. That was my mother's domain. It felt like

I was playing grown up.

"To new beginnings." I said and raised my glass of wine.

"*¡Salud!*" We all clinked glasses.

My mother looked at the menu and I snorted which caught her attention.

"*Ay* shut up!" She said.

"What happened?" Guillermo asked.

I started laughing and she patted me on the arm.

"Mrs. Morales always looks at the menu but orders the same thing each time." Si said.

She looked at both Si and I and although she wanted to look annoyed, she laughed instead.

Hector's eldest daughter Margarita took our order and during the meal, Hector came by with more drinks on the house.

Guillermo worked as an Office Manager for a stationary company. He had noticed my mother during her lunch break at the *cuchifritos* for months before he had the nerve to say hello. He was from The Bronx but moved back to Santurce as a child; where his family were from. He joined the Army when he was 18 and saw the world before settling down in Ponce with his first wife who had died of cancer. He had twin daughters. One was a lesbian who lived in Chicago and the other worked at the US Embassy in Mexico City.

When he spoke I watched my mother hang on his every word. I was happy for her. He did well for himself and he was a gentleman. He opened doors. He stood up from the table when she got up to go to the bathroom, that sort of thing. She deserved that.

"*¿Y qué piensas mijo?*" My mother asked when Guillermo had excused himself to the bathroom.

I looked at Si and then down at the table. I waited till I could see Guillermo coming back towards the table. My mother sat across looking nervous as if my words could make or break the relationship. Guillermo sat down and I looked at him then at her, then back at him.

"I'm really happy for you both." I said. I didn't want to say something awkward like he had my blessing. That was way too *Godfather* without the cat on my lap.

"I'm glad Luis. *Familia es importante* and your approval means everything to us."

They walked us to the subway entrance and it was the first time I didn't feel like I was abandoning my mother for the weekend. They had made plans to go to City Island over the weekend and judging by their body language, I wasn't convinced he was going home that night or the next. I put that out of my head as quick as I could.

My mother gave us both a hug at the same time and said "*Mijos*, don't dance too much." She kissed us each on the cheek.

Si's face turned red. He looked at me and I laughed. "Nice, Lu. Very nice."

"I couldn't resist." He pinched my arm in an affectionate way and then realized where we were. I looked around and no one saw us. I was looking forward to being back downtown.

Guillermo shook my hand and I told him to look after my mother. He then shook Si's hand and asked the same of him. It was that weird kind of male standoff that I didn't get but it was done in a playful way so I went along with it.

When we got on the subway, the tiredness hit me. We were meeting James and Cuchi at Tiffany's although what I wanted to do was head back and watch TV or something. Our knees were touching as the subway car was empty. I was looking forward to holding his hand when we got to the Village.

"He's nice." Si said.

"He does. Mami's happy. I can see that."

Si let out a pleasurable sound sigh. "Happy. I like happy. You happy?"

I put my head on his shoulder for a moment. "I am. You?"

He kissed me on the head. "I am."

We sat back as we were before when then train stopped at Tremont as people got on our car. We sat in silence for most of the journey down to W 4th Street. The closer we got downtown, my energy levels started to rise. The tiredness I had felt when we left the Grand Concourse had lifted as soon as we were out of the subway. The city lights, cabs honking and people going to and from wherever brought me back to life.

I grabbed Si's hand when we walked past The Pink Pussycat. We exchanged grins and I could hear "Domino Dancing" playing from one of the shops.

Tiffany's was busy. Everyone in there looked like they were on their way somewhere. Some to the clubs, others to bar hop all over the Village. Billy and the waitresses looked a bit stressed out as people came out of the restaurant bathrooms transformed for the night. Some in drag, others in club clothes. Dinner with my mother felt like a different night from the world we had just entered and I loved it.

I saw Cuchi in a corner booth with her arms around Rafa. Rafa saw us and waved at us. We walked over and sat with them. Cuchi was in a blonde wig and a black suit, like Madonna in her *Express Yourself* video.

"*Mami*, you look fierce!"

"*Ay Papi*, it's still weird sounding when you say that. *Con* feeling *coño*…FIERCE!"

I repeated it with force but it didn't sound right either.

Si gave them both hugs.

"Where's James?" Si said.

Cuchi rolled her eyes. "I haven't talked to huh in days. You know what bitches are like when they get a man."

"Careful *Mami*, that color might stick." Si said.

Cuchi looked the other way. Billy came over to take our order.

"Coffee." He said. It wasn't a question.

"Thank you Billy." I said.

Rafa leaned over the table as I was sat across the table from him. "I'm sorry, I don't say anything to you at Pelham Bay."

"You see him at Pelham Bay?" Si asked.

"You don't talk to him?" Cuchi said.

I looked at Si. "We take the bus at the same time for the most part. He's at his stop and I'm at mine."

Si sat up.

Rafa was now on the spot.

"I know what it's like up there. I get it. The guys from school would probably beat the shit out of you. It's cool." I said in an attempt to move the conversation along.

Cuchi looked at us both. "How are we going to expect people to see us if we hide?"

"Thank you!" Si said. Both he and Cuchi snapped their fingers.

I turned to Si. "Oh, like when you got scared tonight outside the subway station?"

"That was safety, Lu. C'mon."

"It's the same thing." Rafa had found his voice. "Those guys would fuck me up. They would tell everybody at school, my parents. I don't have cool parents like you and Lu do."

Cuchi put her hands up in the air. "I know you're right but it's not right, that's all I'm saying."

Si was quiet. I reached for his hand.

"You once told me the world is changing, but it hasn't completely."

"I know baby." He held my hand.

"Ooooh child. What did we walk into?" James had arrived with Michael who none of us had expected to see. They were both smiling.

"The state of the world." Cuchi said. She got up and kissed him. She extended her hand to Michael who kissed it. For someone who was in the process of coming out, he made it look so easy.

"Sister Solider over here was telling us how to tear down the system." Rafa said.

I laughed at his queeny remark. It was unexpected but it was perfect and a reminder how things in the Village weren't always what they seemed.

James nodded.

"Where you two been then?" Cuchi said.

"We had some dinner at Empire Szechuan."

"We had Chinese too with Lu's mom and her new boyfriend."

The four of us scooted along so James and Michael could squeeze into the booth with us. There was still a mood between Cuchi and Rafa. The rest of us started talking about going dancing when Cuchi brought us back to the previous conversation.

"What if it was me? Would you talk to me?" Cuchi had her head tilted as if she was ready for a fight.

"That's not a fair question." Rafa said.

The rest of us didn't know where to look. I started feeling like dancing was the furthest thing from my mind, even if it was a great escape from the shit that was happening in the world. I looked to Si for reassurance.

"C'mon, BiGLYNY is tomorrow. The world is a fucked up place for us." Si said. "Lu reminded me that as much as I talk the talk like you Cuchi, we still have to think about our safety. I mean you dress when you come down here. It's like Xavy arrives and Cuchi stays."

James and Michael looked at each other. They were still in date mode judging by their body language. Michael had his hand over James' on the table and though the conversation was serious, they smiled at one another as if they were in their own playground.

Cuchi looked at Rafa. "He's right."

"Not for nothing." Rafa said. "I don't know if I could ignore you even if I tried." He smiled at Cuchi as if he was asking for forgiveness.

"It's a start."

The mood began to lift from there but as I looked around the diner, I realized that I didn't want to be there anymore. It was all too much for me. I wanted to be somewhere totally safe. Yes, it would be cool if Rafa said hello to me after school but I got it. I knew how the world work and I tried not to let it bother me but it did. I hated not holding Si's hand when we weren't in the Village.

"You ok?" Si said in a low voice.

"No. Just thinking about how fucked up it all is. Straight people don't have to have these conversations. They don't worry about saying hello." I looked around the table ad everyone's head was tilted down apart from Cuchi who nodded in agreement. "Why does shit like this have to put a cloud over our night?"

"You know what?" Si said. "Fuck it. Let's go hang at ours tonight. The club will be there another night." He put his arm around me. "Be together in a safe place."

"I know I'd like that." Michael said. His perfect sentences and polite tone stood out in our group and yet it felt right. "I heard there are some dances at Columbia. Maybe I need to try those first before

I'm ready for the clubs."

"That's next week." Cuchi said.

"I've never been to those." I said.

"Cool. Next week Columbia." Si said. "Tonight our place."

We passed Roberta on the stairs up to the apartment. She was dressed in a simple beige coat and black heels. Her hair was up and you could make out a silver necklace clasp against the back of her neck. She looked elegant.

"I didn't know daycare held sleepovers."

"You want to come read us a bedtime story." Cuchi said.

"Honey, my stories would give you nightmares."

"Night Roberta." Si said.

"Good night kids." She said in a soft maternal voice. She continued on her way out, wherever she was headed that time of night.

Fifteen

I headed to Tower Records after work to de stress. Jackie was in a strange mood that afternoon. She was getting ready for a private commission which she hated doing. She thought of them as rich people's Glamour Shots. She was on a double dose of Indigo Girls and if I heard "Galileo" one more time I would have thrown her laptop at her. I was meeting Si after his study group and I still had my birthday money.

I was bopping my head to the music they were playing in the store. The singer sounded familiar but I couldn't place it. She was singing about a couple who sounded like they were arguing. It was catchy.

"Liz Phair."

"Huh." I looked up and there was a guy with a store badge around his neck. He had a pierced lip, nose ring and a very big smile. He was wearing black jeans, ox blood colored Doc Martens and a flannel shirt. I could see a white tank top underneath it. I was surprised how hot I thought he was.

"The music. It's Liz Phair's *Exile to Guyville*. It was released in June."

"Oh okay. Thanks."

He looked me up and down. "You were here last week."

"Um yea." I said. I didn't want to relive the last time I was in the store. It wasn't one of my shining moments and yet it was pretty much how I saw myself more than I cared to admit.

"Thought I recognized you." He pointed to his badge. "I'm Scott. Let me know if you need anything."

"Thanks. I'm Lu."

"Nice to meet you."

"Same."

He continued walking around the shop. I dismissed his niceness as just work. No way he was flirting, *right?* His job was to be friendly so the store could sell more music. I hadn't thought about Liz Phair, but he had sold me on it.

Scott was at the register when I went to pay. I looked at my selection and became self conscious as he rang up Belinda Carlisle's *Real* (which had just been released), Liz Phair, Bjork's *Debut and* Pet Shop Boys' *Very.*

"Nice selection."

I wasn't sure if he was being serious or sarcastic. "Thanks."

I handed him the gift certificate. There was still money left on it after he rang it through.

"Guess I'll see you again, Lu."

I smiled but then felt weird about smiling. *Was I flirting with him? Did I need to tell Si just in case? It's not like Scott was my type. Did I have a type?*

I met Si near the Arch in Washington Square Park. He looked tired but happy to see me.

"*Bon Soir.*" I said.

He smiled. "*Buenas Noches Guapo.*"

I hugged him and kissed him on the cheek.

"Coffee?"

"Yes indeed." He said.

We headed to Espresso Bar. Lamal saw us walk in and had our order rung up by the time we got to the counter. They were playing the Liz Phair album I had just bought. I took that as a sign I made the right choice.

We sat down at one of the high tables against the wall when our drinks were ready.

"So I had some time before we met and I went back to Tower Records."

He perked up with a sip of coffee and leaned in towards me. "What did you get?"

I showed him the CD's. He picked up the Liz Phair and pointed up to the speaker. "Spooky. Now I don't have to buy it." He smiled.

"Well it was recommended by Scott." I said and winked.

"Oh Scott is it."

"Yes. Scott."

"Should I be worried about Scott?"

"Absolutely...NOT." We both laughed. By making a joke of it, the moment at Tower Records didn't feel as awkward as I thought.

He picked up the Belinda Carlisle CD and let out a high pitch sound which made everyone look at us but Si didn't care. His eyes were wide open like a kid on Christmas morning opening presents.

"The new Belinda!!! Even I don't have this yet."

"Nope, but we do."

He put his hand over mine. "You know whenever I hear "Heaven is a Place on Earth," I think of you. I probably always will."

"All her songs remind of me you." I said and took his hand in mine. "Not sure Scott was too impressed with that CD alongside the rest of the ones."

He took another sip of his coffee. "Well, we can't all be as cool as Scott, can we?"

"Guess not."

Since my mother had relaxed her rule about staying over on a school night, our time during the week didn't feel rushed.

"I have some fresh pasta and sauce in the fridge."

"Sounds perfect."

We finished our coffee and strolled home. Arturo was helping out a customer at The Loft and waved at us when he saw us. Bleeker Street was quiet and the lights outside Manatus made the street look like it belonged on a postcard of some New England village. October was only a few days away and there was this feeling in the air that it was time to shut the world out and stay indoors.

Part Two

One

Si wasn't feeling well when we woke up. He had a high temperature and was coughing a lot. I didn't want to leave him alone but as he pointed out, my mother would not be happy about me staying over during the week at his and then missing school. As a compromise, I called his mother and she said to put him in a taxi up to their house.

We rode up together and although we couldn't kiss goodbye, I gave him a long hug after helping him upstairs to his bedroom and promised to call him at lunch.

"I'll get you a car up to school Lu. Thank you." Mrs. Trelawney said as she tucked Si in.

"It's okay Mrs. Trelawney. I can get the subway."

"I insist." She got up and we left Si to rest.

I made it to school just in time for first period. When I walked into Spanish class, Joey shouted out "Girlfriend!" from across the classroom. No one laughed and I felt sorry for him so I snapped my fingers and took my seat which made the class laugh. *What was with that guy?*

At lunch, I was about to call Si when my pager went off with a number I didn't recognize. I called the number in case it was my mother.

"Lu?"

The soft but firm voice was undeniable. "Hi Michael. Everything okay?"

"Yes of course. I was just wondering if you wanted to meet after school."

"Sure."

"Great. Meet me by the McDonalds near the Botanical Gardens."

"Okay."

He hung up and I called Si but he was asleep so I told his mother to have him page me when he was up for talking.

After school, I saw Rafa at the bus stop with his usual group of friends. He looked at me and smiled.

"Hey Lu!"

I stopped where I was and smiled back. "Hey Rafa."

"Who's that?" I heard one of his friends say.

"He's a friend. Mind your own fucking business." He punched the guy in the arm in that way that straight guys did that made no sense to me.

It was a start. He didn't have to say anything and it wouldn't have bothered me, even though it did. But it did make me happy.

I got on the bus and put on the Pet Shop Boys CD I bought. The first track came through my headphones like the Kool-Aid man busting through a wall. "Can You Forgive Her?" It was so obvious the song was about a closet case and it made me laugh. Listening to *Very* on the bus was like being in my own private gay club and it made the journey bearable.

Michael was waiting outside the McDonald's when I got there. In his uniform, he looked even hotter if that was possible. The maroon sweater over his shirt and tie brought out the color of his olive skin and made his eyes a brighter blue. As soon as he saw me, he dropped his cigarette and walked towards me.

"Sorry. Some of my classmates are in there." He said. "Can we walk?" He put his hand on my shoulders in that way brothers did.

We crossed back towards where the bus had dropped me off and walked further down as if we were heading towards the main entrance to the New York Botanical Gardens. We stopped halfway down the street where it was empty. He gave me a boost so I could get onto the top of the iron gates and I jumped down from there. He was tall and strong enough to lift himself up. He made it look like the easiest thing in the world. We walked into the pine forest and sat down on a bed of dried pine needles. It was peaceful. We had a perfect view of the traffic and roads with only a humming sound coming from them.

He reached into his cigarette pack, pulled out a half smoked joint and lit it. He took a deep hit and passed it onto me. I took a very small hit as I didn't want to be too stoned when I got home. I passed it back to him.

"Sorry about that back there with the classmates stuff."

I patted his shoulder. "I get it. Don't worry."

He took another hit. "Thanks, Lu."

"So what's up?" I said.

He took a deep breath. "I like James a lot. When we're together downtown, there is nowhere else I could imagine being." He looked out towards the traffic as if he were searching for words.

"That's great though. He's amazing and you guys make a cute couple."

"Thing is." He said. "We're from two different worlds and I don't know."

"But isn't that exciting too?"

He looked at me and I could see in his face that my response was simple but he wasn't buying it either.

"My life feels very disconnected right now."

There it was. The real reason he was feeling the way he did. It was that feeling we all had when we first started to come out. When we find other people like ourselves. When we have to lie to our parents and hide a part of ourselves from the world. I patted him on the shoulder and he leaned into me. He reminded me of a little kid who just needed to be told that he was okay, that it was the world that had the problem.

"Just a part of who we are." I said. "We get to that point where we can be honest with ourselves but it doesn't end there. We then have to be honest with the world and it doesn't end there either. I don't know if it ever ends but I do know that having friends around you helps. It helps a lot."

He smiled at my words.

"A boyfriend?"

"That hasn't hurt either." I said. "But Si is also my best friend." I hadn't verbalized it until that moment but he was. He was the one that I wanted to speak too first.

"That's beautiful Lu." He put his arm around me and pulled me towards him in a playful way. "Thanks for this."

"Anytime."

We sat a bit longer in a comfortable silence. I had only done that before with Si but this was different. It wasn't like I felt I wanted to touch Michael or be with him in anyway. It felt like a friendship had begun and it was nice to know that I didn't have to always go downtown to hang out with a friend.

I walked Michael to the Metro-North station at Fordham and he gave me a hug before going down to the platform. I carried on walking up Fordham Road and stopped into Kentucky Fried Chicken because I had the munchies.

Si was feeling a little better when we spoke that night. I told him about my afternoon.

"You're a good friend." He said.

"You're my best friend." I said.

"That's the best thing I have heard all day." He coughed. "I miss you baby."

"I do too."

We spoke as long as he was able to. He didn't want to get me sick so he decided to stay at his parents for a few days and we would see each other on Friday. My mother was in a happy mood as she served up dinner and if she knew I was a bit stoned, she didn't say anything but she did giggle and shake her head when I had a second plate of *chuletas.*

Two

Melanie *fucking* Sputano was also becoming a friend and as strange as it was, it was also nice to have someone at school I could talk to. I didn't tell her that I had seen Michael. He had paged me again that morning to thank me for the chat and that he was looking forward to hanging out on Friday.

We were sat outside the auditorium just under the shade of a tree. It was sunny that day and in direct sunlight, it felt like summer had come back.

"So Michael is really into that black guy huh?" She said.

"James? His name is James." I said and rolled my eyes. "I think they're into each other." I knew she was trying but her ignorance could really get on my nerves at times.

"Huh."

My beeper went off. It was Si. I excused myself and went to the pay phone across the street. It was a welcomed break from what had turned into an awkward moment with Melanie. Given our history, it wasn't the first nor would it be the last one I was sure.

"Hey baby." Hi voice was low and coarse. He was struggling to speak.

"You don't sound too great. Anything I can do?"

"Just let me hear your voice." He coughed.

I felt those butterflies flutter in my stomach. "I miss you."

"I miss you too."

"I hope you're okay by the weekend. You do remember what the weekend is?"

"Four months." He said. "I promise we'll do something together."

"Just get better."

"Call me later?"

"You got it."

When I got back to Mel, she was smiling at me. "You get this glow when you talk to your boyfriend."

"Say it louder, I don't think they heard you in Country Club." I looked around to see if anyone had started to look at us. Even though I was out at school it was a force of habit to feel on guard.

"Oh shut up Lu. You got nothing to be ashamed of it and it's nice to see you glow." She got up and gave me a hug. "I hope I find someone who makes me glow like that."

I looked at her. "You will."

"You think?"

"Well after Anthony, c'mon."

She laughed and slapped me on the chest. "Don't be a bitch!!"

Jackie paged me that afternoon to tell me that she was stuck in Sag Harbor and that if I could stop by the following day instead. I thought about heading downtown anyway but as much fun as it was to hang out with James and Cuchi, I really wanted to see Si so instead, I decided I would head home after Jackie's. The quicker he got better, the sooner I could see him. It was still warm outside and instead of taking the bus to Pelham Bay, I walked. I put Liz Phair on my CD player and enjoyed the relative peace of the streets until I passed George's Restaurant near Buhre Avenue station and saw Joey. He snapped his fingers at me. I gave him side eye and continued walking. *Honestly, what the fuck was with that guy?*

Rafa was at the bus stop again but he was alone. He waved me over and when I got there, he gave me this firm handshake which was such an obvious straight boy move that it made me cringe until I remembered that it only felt that way because I knew the truth. To everyone around us, it would look totally normal.

"You got time for a walk?"

I shrugged. With Jackie having cancelled on me and Si being sick, I had more time than I cared to admit.

We headed into Pelham Bay Park in the direction of the War Memorial as if we were walking towards Orchard Beach and City Island.

"You know the first time I was ever with a guy was in this park?" Rafa said.

"Oh." I didn't know what else to say.

"Yea. It was over the summer. It was my brother's friend Mike. We had both missed the bus and it was a hot day so we decided to you know fuck it and walk to City Island." He smiled as he said it. "If a bus came on the way then we'd hop on it. Anyway, as we walked, we both started to sweat so we took our shirts off and walked like that." He giggled. "When we crossed the bridge just up here, I had to pee so I ducked into bushes and Mike followed. After I finished peeing, I noticed Mike was still standing there and playing with himself. I got turned on by the whole thing and you know next thing we're playing with each other."

"Wow." I hadn't expected to hear that or even knew why he was opening up to me. What I did know was that he needed to tell someone because of the tone of his voice. "What happened to Mike?" I said.

It took Rafa a minute to answer my question. He had this look like he was trying to remember every detail of that encounter. As if he was searching his memory for something. "Huh?" He said. "Oh, he's a freshman at Stonybrook." Rafa then looked as if he had found what he was scanning his memory for. "You know he never talked to me after that. Fucked up huh?"

"Some guys aren't ready to face up to who they are?"

"Yea I guess." He said. "What about you?"

"Si was my first."

He stopped walking. "Really?"

I smiled. "Yea. He was my first kiss. My first everything." I knew I wasn't Si's first and I knew most guys my age weren't with their firsts. It didn't bother me. As lame as it sounded, I was happy that Si was my first. He still made me feel like I was the only person in the world that mattered. It must say something that we're going on four months and we still feel that way, right?

"That's beautiful." I hadn't noticed how strong his Bronx accent was until he said the word *beautiful*. "Do you think it's weird that I don't mind if I'm with Cuchi or Xavy?"

"What do you mean?" We continued walking.

"Well, you know I still like girls and with Cuchi and Xavy, I sort of get both."

I thought about what he said for a moment and I wasn't sure he understood that Cuchi was a drag queen and not a transsexual. I decided to let Xavy or Cuchi handle that conversation. I could hear the crunch of the dried leaves under my feet as we walked.

"I think it's great that you accept them both."

"I think I might be in love." He said. "I don't know what to do about that."

I didn't entirely know what to say or why he was opening up to me but whatever it was, I just listened.

"How did you know you were in love with Si?"

"I don't know. I guess it's because when I think about him, I feel it in my stomach. When I hear his voice, it makes me feel like I'm flying." I looked up at a bird flying by. "When we're together, I feel complete."

"You're lucky." He bumped into me and smiled.

"I think we're all lucky." I bumped back into him and it was one of those playful ones. Not the secret kissing as Si and I called it, more like what guys do when they are sharing moment they don't want other guys to know about.

"What do you mean?"

"We're all lucky to have found each other. As friends, boyfriends, whatever."

He stopped walking and gave me a big hug which took me by surprise. Not that it was a weird hug, just didn't expect it but then I hadn't expected anything that afternoon. *Was I making another friend in The Bronx?*

Rafa decided to walk the rest of the way to City Island. I headed back to Pelham Bay to catch the bus home. I stopped off at a pay phone before the bus stop because I wanted to hear Si's voice. I took the chance that he might be up and able to talk. When he picked up, I could hear "Circle in the Sand" playing in the background.

"VH1 is showing an 80's countdown."

"I was I was there."

"THAT would make Heaven." He said. "A place on Earth." He laughed and coughed.

It may have been cheesy to some, but Belinda Carlisle was our thing. It had been our thing since we met and it didn't matter what anyone else thought. That too was our thing.

Three

I had agreed with my mom that Friday after school I would pick up Si and take him home as the novelty of staying with his parents had worn off and he felt well enough that he wasn't contagious. Since our weekly dinner was Friday, we decided the night before to have a pizza and video night just the two of us.

When I walked into the kitchen, she was putting the leftover pizza in the fridge. She was humming "I Feel Pretty." I watched her for a moment before she was aware I had entered.

"I always thought "America" was your favorite?" I said.

She kicked her leg up like Rita Moreno in the film. "*Sí, claro pero*" she looked over at the empty Jiffy Pop pan on the stove and then back at me. "His favorite too, *y tuyo tambien.*"

Uncle Jose loved musicals and whenever we watched them together, he always made popcorn. I walked over to her and gave her a hug.

"We should go visit his grave soon?" I said.

She smiled. "*Sí amor.* Let's do it."

"You seeing Guillermo tonight?"

She nodded.

"Good. I don't want you to be alone."

"*Nunca.*" She said and squeezed my cheeks.

There was a substitute teacher that day for my last period, so I cut class and headed downtown. All day the only thought in my head was being able to see Si. This had been the longest we had gone without seeing each other since we first met. I could feel myself being pulled towards him like a magnet as the train sped downtown. It was going to take forever to get to his parents by subway so I got off at 86th Street and took a taxi cross town.

Mr. Trelawney was loading their Jeep with some bags when the taxi pulled up. By the time I had paid the taxi and got out of it, Mrs. Trelawney had appeared with a suitcase for Mr. Trelawney to put in the back of the Jeep.

"Hi Mr. & Mrs. Trelawney"

"Alright Lu."

"Ah Lu. How are you my dear?" Mrs. Trelawney gave me a kiss on both cheeks. She was in good spirits, most likely because they were heading to their weekend place.

"How's the patient?"

"Better but I wish he would come to the country with us." She threw her hands up. "But he insists on staying in the city."

I left them to continue packing the Jeep and went up to Si's bedroom. I leant against the doorframe. He was bent over putting some clothes and books into a backpack. The top off his underwear was visible just under his loose fitting green jeans; He was barefoot and wearing a black t-shirt that was the right fit. It wasn't tight. It was perfect on him. On the TV, "November Rain" by Guns n Roses was playing on VH1. It seemed they were always playing it on that channel, *or was it just me?*

I could hear Si singing along to it.

"Hey hot stuff."

He stood up straight, turned around and smiled from ear to ear. His nose was a bit red from the cold and you could tell he was still tired but he walked as fast as he could towards me. He wrapped his arms around me and I had to catch myself from falling over.

"God, I have missed you!" He said. His voice was not quite back to normal but he sounded better than he had earlier on the phone.

I took in the smell of the Garnier shampoo that his parents liked to buy and the fresh scent of the Calvin Klein soap on a rope that I knew he kept at his parents.

"I've missed you too. How are you feeling?"

He looked me in the eyes and blinked once in a slow affectionate way. "Better now."

I helped Si finish packing his bag and he shut the TV off as Blind Melon's "No Rain" began to play. When we got outside, we said goodbye to his parents and Mr. Trelawney slipped twenty dollars into my hand.

"Take a cab downtown, okay?"

"No probs." I said.

Si gave both his parents long hugs and I heard him say *thanks* to them both for looking after him. They made me promise to call them if he got worse. We waved them off.

"I'm ready to go home baby. What about you?"

I picked up his bag so that he didn't have to carry it. "Let's go."

We walked down to Columbus Avenue and hailed a taxi from

there. Si sunk into the back seat and closed his eyes as we headed downtown. I held his hand and for the first time that week, I felt whole again. I had a feeling he would crawl into bed when we got home but that didn't matter because we would be together.

Roberta was coming out of the building as our taxi pulled up. She stopped and bent down to look at us as I paid the driver and then opened the door. She watched in silence as we got out of the taxi. She then turned her head sideways.

"Hi Roberta." Si said. His voice had become raspy since we had left his parents house.

"Uh uh Typhoid Mary. You stay back." She then winked and kept walking.

We both laughed. Si held his chest as if he was uncomfortable. Her lack of tact and dismissive attitude was funny but we knew that underneath it all, Roberta was a compassionate woman. It was there in her eyes.

When we got upstairs, I settled Si on the sofa so he could rest. I brought him the comforter from the futon and wrapped it around him. I made him some hot lemon tea with honey and put it on the coffee table.

"You're good to me." He said. His head was sticking out from under the green comforter and he looked like a dirty blonde caterpillar. His eyes were half opened and he had a grin which made me smile.

"We're good together." I said. I gave him a kiss on the forehead and he nodded.

I put the TV on and there was a re-run of *The Real World* on. Si seemed pleased with that as he turned on his side to watch it. I went into the kitchen to have a look at what food we had left. I wasn't too hopeful given that neither of us had been there all week. The milk had expired and the leftover pasta from our last dinner together had started to smell.

I went into the living room and Si looked as if he was asleep. I went up to him and whispered in his ear that I was going to the supermarket.

"Can you get Jell-O? He said without opening his eyes.

"You got it."

I walked up to Gristedes on Sheridan Square. It was a beautiful Fall evening. Not too cold, just a slight breeze in the air that made you put your jacket collar up to protect your neck. The city felt like it had slowed down since the summer. *Maybe it was the weather that kept most people indoors? Maybe people just walked further apart and at a slower pace?*

Gristedes was busy with the after work crowd, mainly guys in suits who cruised one another while putting their nightly groceries in their baskets. It was a playful sight to watch. The look down to the floor just after making eye contact, pretending to read the ingredients of something as if they weren't interested; before looking back and smiling. I had become used to watching the dance and it was a reminder of how where I grew up; and the Village were worlds apart. I picked up some milk, Jell-O, tortilla chips, Chi- Chi's salsa, bread, cheese and a couple of cans of Campbell's Cream of Tomato Soup. Uncle Jose used to make me grilled cheese sandwiches and tomato soup when I was sick and I thought Si might appreciate it. I was heading towards the cashier when I heard a voice that sounded familiar.

"You liking that Liz Phair?"

It was Scott.

"Huh. Oh hi. Yea, I am. Thanks."

"Another satisfied customer." He licked his upper lip a bit as he spoke.

"Scott, you get the salsa?" Said another voice from behind him.

"One sec." He then looked at me. "Gotta go. See you around. I hope."

"Sure." I said. I was happy that the conversation had been cut short. I looked over to see who had called him and I couldn't believe my eyes. I tried not to laugh. It was Jamie. I couldn't wait to tell Si. Jamie looked a bit embarrassed when he saw me until he looked at Scott and then back at me.

"Oh you." Jamie said. "Haven't seen Si, your boyfriend, all week." He sounded so bitchy and bitter that I almost felt sorry for him.

"He's sick." I said and lifted my basket. "Going to make him grilled cheese and tomato soup." I smiled.

Scott laughed at my response but not in a making fun kind of way. It was like he was laughing at the tension between Jamie and me. Maybe even laughing at how I handled it. Jamie put his arm around Scott.

"Tell him I hope he feels better." He then half smiled and led Scott towards the cashier.

"Later dude." Scott said and winked at me.

When I got home, Si was sat up and laughing at an episode of *The Golden Girls*. He smiled at me as I walked through the door.

"You should be resting."

"Apartment felt empty without you."

"Outside was weird without you." I put the groceries in the kitchen and then told him about Jamie and Scott which made him laugh. I left him on the sofa while I made his strawberry Jell-O, and then the soup and grilled cheese.

"This is the best." He said after dipping his grilled cheese sandwich into a bowl of soup. "Total comfort food."

After eating, we cuddled on the sofa and watched *The X-Files* video that his dad had given us. His dad was recording each week as it was becoming his new favorite show. The closeness is what I missed the most that week we were apart. Si was in my arms, half dozing. He had a grin on his face and he squeezed my arm as he adjusted himself so that there was no space between us. I was happy to lay there all night with him when I heard my beeper go off.

I reached over him and looked at the number. It was Xavy. I had forgotten that we were all supposed to go to the Columbia Dance that night. It was the furthest thing from my mind after I picked Si up that afternoon.

"Shit."

Si opened his eyes. "Huh. What? Everything ok?"

"Oh yea. It's Xavy." I said. "Totally forgot we were supposed to go to Columbia Dance tonight."

Si wrapped his arms around me.

"I'll let them know that we're not up for it."

"You should go." He said. "I'm feeling like crap and to be honest, I'd rather sleep so I can enjoy the weekend."

"No. It wouldn't be the same." I said.

"Well of course not." He smiled and let out a cough. "But honestly, it's not a problem."

"You sure?" I asked.

"Of course, baby." He put his arms around me. "I'll be here waiting for you when you get home."

"Okay but only if you're sure."

He let out a frustrated sound. "Lu, I wouldn't say it, if I didn't mean it."

I kissed him on the lips.

"Call him back before he blows up your beeper." Si said. "You know what he's like."

My beeper went off again and we both laughed.

I called Xavy back and we agreed to meet outside 116th Street subway station near Columbia University. It was the first time we had all been together where I was the odd one out. Xavy and Rafa were together, so was James and Michael. We headed towards Earl Hall, where the dance was.

I had been to gay bars, clubs and even dances at The Center but this felt more like a college party than an actual dance. Even though it was open to everyone, I felt out of place but not because we were made to feel out of place. I felt out of place because I wasn't used to going out without Si. As we headed to the coat check, it felt like all eyes were on us. Although when you looked closer, more eyes were on Michael. I could tell in James' face that he knew it and he wore it with pride. He had his arm around Michael and looked at the room with batted eyelashes as if he was saying, *all mine bitches*. Michael I could tell was less comfortable with the fresh meat look. In the short time I had known him, I was certain that he wasn't as comfortable with his looks as other people were with them.

We headed to the dance floor which was busy but not so crowded that we couldn't all dance together. The DJ was playing "I'm Every Woman" by Whitney Houston. Although, Si wasn't there, the group didn't let me feel like I was alone. I lost myself in the mimicking, the hand pointing and the beat of the music. The DJ continued to play uplifting music like Robin S, Crystal Waters, Donna Summer and Gloria Gaynor, which made everyone join in and sing along to. Through the crowd I saw Scott smiling at me. I shook my head and continued dancing with Xavy and Rafa. Scott grinned at me and I saw Xavy look at him and then at me. I shrugged it off.

Michael and James wanted a cigarette so we all went outside. The chill in the air dried the sweat on my body and even though it felt a bit clammy after, there was a split second relief. James and Michael were stood in their own world and it was nice to watch. Xavy and

Rafa were also talking and looking as if they didn't want to be disturbed. I sat down on the stairs and looked up at the clear sky. The campus was quiet apart from the bass coming from upstairs of Earl Hall. It still got me how busy the city was and yet how you could find parts where if you were to record the sounds, nothing. *Would anyone believe you were in New York if you heard nothing?*

"Hey Lu."

I looked at the stair and I could see the ox blood Doc Martens just inches from my Converse.

"Hey Scott."

"I take it the soup and the grilled cheese wasn't enough to make the boyfriend feel well enough to come out tonight?" He said and offered me one of his Camel Lights.

"No thanks." I said. "Where's Jamie?"

"At home studying or out at a bar." He lit his cigarette. "We do our own things sometimes. You know what it's like?"

"What what's like?"

He let out a laugh and took a drag. He looked at me but I wasn't laughing with him.

"Oh. Right. I guess I just thought most guys our ages had open relationships."

"Maybe." I shrugged my shoulders. "Not us though."

He shook his head as he smoked. "Been together long?"

"Four months tomorrow." I said. It felt good to say it out loud. I was proud of that.

"Honeymoon period. Give it time."

"And you?" I chose to ignore his snide comment.

"About a year." He said. He took another drag and then put his cigarette out under his left foot. "Is Si off to Paris like Jamie is next year?"

I turned my body towards him. "Paris? What do you mean about Paris?" Apart from it being where Si was born, Paris hadn't come up in any conversation we'd had.

"Oh." He said as he smiled.

I was about to ask him again when Xavy interrupted us.

"*Papi*. Can I talk to you?"

"Sure." I was happy for the interruption. "Excuse me." I said to Scott.

Xavy gave him a look worthy of Cuchi. It was like he was setting the space between Scott and me on fire and cleansing the immediate area around it. We walked around the building away from everyone.

"*Papi*. You need to watch yourself. Guys like that will always try it with you. I see you, you like the attention. Who wouldn't? *Pero* don't fuck it up for a cheap self esteem fix."

"I wouldn't cheat on Si."

Xavy pulled a cigarette out of his pack and lit it. "Gurl, I know you wouldn't cos you know I would beat your ass for being a *pendeja*." He took a drag and exhaled. "*Mira*, guys can always tell when you're happy and they want that." He pointed his cigarette in my direction. "They want that shit like its heroin and they'll do anything to get a hit. ¿*Sabes?*

His words made perfect sense. Why did Scott mention Paris? Why put that in my head? What was the point of telling me about his arrangement? What was he trying to prove?

"You're right."

"I know bitch." He gave me a hug and I held him tight.

"What would I do without you?"

"May you never find out."

Xavy finished his cigarette and we returned to the group who were ready to go back inside and continue dancing. Scott was nowhere to be seen and I was happy about that.

Four

"Happy Monthaversary Baby." Si said as he put his hand on my chest.

I was just waking up and the touch of his cold hand caused me to jump. I turned on my side to look at him. The color had returned to his face and his eyes were brighter. Seeing him smile and being able to press our naked bodies against each other made me happy that we could celebrate our monthaversary.

"Happy Monthaversary." I pushed a strand of hair away from his face. "You look better."

"I feel better." He said and kissed my lips.

The only sound in the room was from birds in the trees outside the window. The room was calm.

"Coffee?"

He kissed me again. "Oh yea. I'll make it."

"No, you rest. I'll make it."

He got up before I could and the blanket fell off him revealing his beautiful smooth ass. I whistled and he smacked his right cheek, looked back and winked at me. There was no doubt that he was feeling better.

I got up and followed him to the kitchen. When I caught up with him, I put my arms around his waist and he leant back into me. He grabbed my hand and kissed it.

"Well, I was going to ask what you wanted to do today but I think

I have an idea."

He turned around put his hands on my waist. He arched his eyebrows and I kissed him on the lips. We went back to the bedroom. The coffee could wait a little longer.

Whatever doubts I had that past week or weirdness that had happened with Scott had disintegrated. We laid afterwards in each other's arms. The room smelled of us. A week had felt a lifetime but the distance had faded and I was so happy to have Si back.

"Hey, I got something for you." I said and got up from the futon. I walked over to the dresser and reached behind it. I had taped his gift to the back of it so he wouldn't find it.

Si had propped himself up on his elbow when I got back to bed. I put the slim black box with small red cloth bow in front of him and lay on my side so I could watch him open it.

He looked at me and then down at the box. He took the lid off and then tipped the contents into his hand. It was a silver chunky linked bracelet with a small medallion hanging off it that made it look like a charm bracelet. He looked at the medallion and smiled as he read it: "L & S 06.03.93."

Si held it in his hand and rubbed his finger around it. He then opened the bracelet and held it against his skin. The shiny metallic effect sparkled against his golden skin from the summer months.

"Do you like it?"

"I love it." He pushed me down on the futon and kissed me hard. He reached over me and pulled something from under the futon.

"For you."

He put an envelope on my chest and propped himself up again. I took the envelope and opened it. There was a thick hand-made card inside. On the front of the card was a picture of us taken not too longer after we had gotten together. I was sat with my back against one of the barriers on the pier. Si's head was on my lap and I was looking down at him while he looked up at me. I think James had taken the photo. It was beautiful and took me back to that hot day.

Si had a day off of work and I met him after school to hang out on the piers. We hadn't made plans to meet anyone else but it didn't matter. On a hot day, where else would everyone end up? We ran into Cuchi and James. It was one of those days that came to define the summer yet to come. There were people drinking, smoking, music playing, and queens' voguing against each other. The city was alive around us and the piers beat with its rhythm.

I opened the card. Inside, written in smooth cursive script that made me think of old fashioned love letters was: "A weekend in the country. Just the two of us."

I looked up at him surprised. "You mean a weekend getaway?"

He nodded his head. "My parents are letting us use their house one weekend this month."

I screamed in excitement and threw my arms around him.

"You like then?"

"I love." I said. "I love you!"

He held me tight. "I love you too."

"Shall we have that coffee now?" I said.

He kissed me and we got up. Si put the coffee maker on while I looked for some music to play. I chose Belinda Carlisle's *Runaway Horses* album. It was the perfect choice for us. The conversation with Scott crept back into my head as "Leave a Light On" began to play. I didn't want to make a big deal about it but I didn't want it in my head either.

Si returned with our cups and I looked up at him from the sofa as he hummed along.

"You okay?" He said.

I took a deep breath. The smell of hazelnut coffee came up from my cup and I took a sip. "I ran into that Scott guy at the dance last night." I said. "Did you know he and Jamie have an open relationship?"

He shrugged and looked at me a little confused. "Big deal. Lots of people do. Nothing wrong with it." He looked down at his cup and took a sip.

The mood had become tense.

"I know. Thing is, I think he was trying to get into my head. He said something about how I felt about you going to Paris."

Si put his cup down and then put his hands on my knee. He looked at me and I could see that he was not prepared for what I had said and even less so that day.

"I haven't decided if I am applying for the month in Paris."

"Oh." I sat up. I hadn't prepared for Scott to be right. I thought he had said that to fuck with my head or to get Si and me to break up or to get me into bed. I didn't know what to say. "Runaway Horses" was playing in the background.

He squeezed my knee. "Baby, look at me. Please?"

I faced him and his look must have been a reflection of mine. How had we gone from such a hot start to our monthaversary to that?

"It's a great opportunity but I also know that the thought of that time apart, drives me crazy." He took a deep breath. "Mum said I should talk to you before I make a decision and then I got sick."

"Wait, is that what you and her were talking about that Sunday?"

He nodded.

"So you've been keeping this from me all that time?"

"No baby." He put his arm around me and I could feel him shaking. "If anything, I have been trying not to think about it. She was pushing me that weekend about it and it was only when I was home sick that we talked about it and that she understood where I was coming from."

I leaned into him. It was my turn to not want to think about it. Even though he wasn't leaving for sure, it was there. That question: Paris? It was supposed to be our happy day. I didn't want to feel that way.

"Can we put it out of our heads today?" I said. I wasn't sure I could but I wanted to try.

He half smiled. "Yes. Talk about it soon though, ok? Promise?"

I agreed and put my arms around him as Belinda sang on. I held him tight like the song went.

We finished our coffee, got dressed and headed to The Waverley for breakfast. We talked about everything else but Paris, although Paris was there. I couldn't even order the French Toast which was my favorite. I went for chocolate chip pancakes because chocolate made me feel better. Paris also made me think about the other thing that hung between us that we hadn't spoken about. *What was I going to do about college? Something else I hadn't wanted to think about.* I wanted more chocolate after breakfast so we stopped off at Caffe Raffiella and got some cake to go. The day was gray and the rain was on and off. I just wanted to be close to Si and since we had our own place, at least we could do that. *Maybe if we were in bed naked, Paris and college would cease to exist?*

I called my mother when we got back to tell her I was staying the night. I knew she would be okay with it; I just wanted to hear her voice. I could hear Guillermo in the background and put it out of my head as quick as the thought had entered. By the time I had gotten off the phone, Si had lit some candles and had put the cake on one plate with two forks on the coffee table. He was sat crossed legged waiting for me. Walking towards him, the questions circled in my head: Could we survive the distance? Could we be together even if we didn't see each other? Was that even considered being together?

I sat next to him as close as I could.

"You can't stop thinking about it. Can you?" Si said.

"That obvious?"

"I know you Lu."

He didn't sound annoyed though. He uncrossed his legs so he

could get closer. There was almost no room between us and he put pulled me closer so the space pretty much disappeared.

"Talk to me?"

"Paris made me think about college applications."

He touched my face and smiled. "The other elephant in the room."

"Do you think we could survive not seeing each other?"

He sighed and I could see the sadness in his eyes. I could feel it in my chest.

"I know that I would rather try than not be with you at all.

"Really?"

"Yea. Of course. You?"

He hadn't said anything that I shouldn't have known in my heart but hearing the words made me jump inside. I felt like all was not lost.

"Yes. Of course!"

I dug my head into his chest.

"Whatever we decide, we support each other, okay? Whatever it is, we talk. No more, not mentioning shit."

I got up from the sofa and extended my hand to him.

"Deal?"

He got up and we kissed. The room became lighter and I was ready to continue our monthaversary. I walked towards the bedroom and he smiled.

"Don't forget the cake." I said.

In the middle of the night, I got up to use the bathroom and decided to smoke a cigarette on the fire escape. It was cold and I wrapped myself up in my bathrobe. Across the street, the lights were on in one of the apartments. A gay couple sat at a dining table with Chinese food containers between them. They were smiling and laughing as they ate with chopsticks. I watched them as I smoked. I loved watching couples interact when they thought no one was watching them. You got a glimpse into how they really were with each other. I started to feel at ease. Si and I would be alright. We could get through anything. We could be stronger from it. I finished my cigarette and climbed back in.

"You okay?" Si was standing by the bedroom door.

"I am."

He held his arms open and I walked towards them. He squeezed me tight and we went back to bed. I don't remember what I dreamt about or if I dreamt at all. All I know is that when I woke up in Si's arms, it was the perfect start to the week.

Five

"Girl, you two are gonna be just fine." James said to me. He was behind the counter putting price labels on some boxes of *Incense of the West*. Carol had left him in the shop to close up that night.

I should have gone right home after Jackie's but I needed to talk to someone and James was the most levelheaded out of all of us. You could tell him anything and he wouldn't be surprised or judgmental.

"Anyway, it's good to talk about it." He said. He put the labels down and looked me in the eyes. "If you're meant to be together, you will." He smiled.

"You really believe that?"

"Look at where I work." He held his hands up. "Of course I believe it."

"What about you and Michael?"

"It is what it is." He said. "I like him. I don't know where this train is gonna end up." He smiled. "But I'm enjoying the ride."

I laughed and clapped my hands as he moved his hips in a playful way.

"Thanks." I said.

"What are friends for, *Papi*?" He then picked up the price tags and continued putting them on the boxes.

I left Stick, Stone and Bone and walked up to The Loft. Arturo was working. He was hanging up packages of Calvin Klein underwear and moving his hip to Madonna's "La Isla Bonita." I popped in to invite him to visit Uncle Jose's grave with us the following Saturday. Si, Cuchi and James had already confirmed and it felt right for Arturo to be there too given their history. If things had been different, he would have been my Uncle too. Who knows, maybe Uncle Jose would have still been with us.

"Yes, of course." Arturo said with his hand on his chest. "*Amor*, thank you."

I gave him a huge hug. A customer walked in which stopped our conversation. I was glad of it though, as I could feel myself choking up inside and my head filling with all sorts of sad thoughts.

I walked at a slower pace than I usually did, taking in the Village. There were fewer footsteps and more car sounds. The sidewalk wasn't busy like it was in the summer when Christopher Street felt like a runway of people showing their goods and smiles. Paris didn't seem so bad and although I was still no closer to wanting to think about college, that too didn't seem so bad. I was about to cross 7th Avenue South when I ran into Si.

"Hey baby." He said smiling. "What are you doing down here?"

"I just needed to talk to Arturo about the cemetery." I said. I didn't mention my chat with James.

He put his arms around me.

"A bite to eat before you head back?"

I kissed him on the lips. I thought I heard someone yell. "Fags!" But in his arms, I wasn't afraid. I felt safe. We held hands as we walked up to The Waverley. We sat up on the elevated part of the diner in a booth against the wall towards the counter. The waitress brought us some water and we both ordered coffee. Si held my hand across the table with this look that made me feel like I was the only person in the room. As much as I should have told him I would be downtown, running into him on the street was even better. It was bonus time. It was a gift.

The waitress came back with our coffee and took our orders. Si's expression hardened when he looked down at the far corner near the entrance to the diner.

"One sec baby." He said and got up.

I looked over and saw Jamie and Scott sat there. They had taken notice of us and from Si's expression, he wasn't happy.

Jamie stood up and smiled as Si went up to them.

"Hey Man." I heard Jamie say.

"This is for both of you." Si said. "I don't give a fuck what arrangement you two have but you see that guy up there." He pointed to me and I could feel everyone in the diner look at me. "Nothing is coming between us and if we chose it, it certainly wouldn't be either of you."

Si didn't even wait for a response. He walked back towards me and passed a woman sitting in the next booth who clapped.

"That's right!" She said out loud so that the whole diner turned their attention to her. "Can't stand a home wrecker!"

I looked over at Jamie and Scott who put money on the table and left as fast as they could. Given their body language, I was sure they were heading for an argument.

I was turned on by what had just happened. He stood up for me.

He stood up for us. *Of course we could survive anything,* I thought to myself when he sat back down across from me. I put my hand over his and I could feel his love through his hand and the look in his eyes.

"I wish I didn't have to go home tonight."

"Then don't." He said and squeezed my hand.

"I have homework to do."

"I have reading to do."

He kept his eyes fixated on me with a grin that I couldn't resist. None of what he had said was wrong. I got up and went to the pay phone to call my mother. She didn't pick right up away and when she did, she was a bit out of breath.

"*Si mijo,* fine." She said and hung up before I could say anything.

I stood there for a moment with the phone in my hand and decided it was best not to think about it any further.

When we got back to our apartment, Si made some more coffee and put on a Miles Davis CD. We sat opposite each other at the dining table. He was reading one of his French history textbooks. I worked on my English essay. It was on *The Scarlet Letter.* We stole glances from time to time and played a subtle game of footsies. I started to think that this was a possibility. We could study and be together at the same time. That we could support each other and that our relationship could take on a whole new dimension. *Were we entering a new level in our relationship?*

Six

Mrs. Mallory, the guidance counselor had a raspy voice from too many cigarettes. If they used her on anti-smoking commercials, I was pretty sure no one would smoke. She hunched over my file as if she was trying to find mistakes and muttered to herself as she read before she looked up at me and half smiled.

"Luis. Your grades are good enough but what do you want to study?"

I shrugged.

She took her glasses off and put them on the desk. She held her hands and tapped her thumbs together.

"Alright. What do you like to do?"

"I like reading and writing."

"Good, okay." She said. "That's a start." She coughed. "Maybe a teacher? Maybe a journalist?"

"They sound good."

She shook her head and I could see in her facial expression she was less than impressed.

"I'm going to level with you Luis. You need direction."

"That's why I am here."

"Come to the college fair next week." She then dismissed me with her hand. The whole experience was surreal. I kept thinking about English as a degree but then what do you do with that? As much as my mother wanted me to be happy, I'm sure she also wanted me to find a job.

Later that afternoon at Jackie's I asked her opinion.

"College is bullshit." She said with a glass of red wine in her hand. "Loads of debt, you'll never be able to pay off. My advice, have fun, do drugs, you'll hear your calling when you're ready."

"What about you?"

She put her wine down and lit a cigarette.

"What about me?" She said. "I was born a photographer. College didn't teach me that." She thought about it again. "It did teach me never to move in with the girl that gives you crabs."

I laughed.

"It's not funny Lu. Took me ages to get rid of them."

I wasn't sure she was being completely honest with herself or me about what college taught her but the conversation was worth it just for the laughs. I was pretty sure that my mother wouldn't have the same take on college that Jackie had. She did though think it was mature of Si and me to support each other whatever decision we made.

"I could learn a thing or two from you two. Very adult."

I told my mother about my conversation with Mrs. Mallory over dinner that night. She made Spaghetti and meatballs which was one of my favorite dishes. I'm pretty sure the Italians would have shunned her for using *adobo* and *sazón* as seasoning but then it didn't matter, she used them on everything.

"*Ella tiene razón*, you do need direction." She said as she sliced a meatball in half with her fork. "And more than just where Simon is."

I ignored her comment.

"She said I should write down all the things I like to do."

My mother nodded her head.

I washed the dishes after we ate and I called Si.

"It's not a bad idea." He said. "My mother is a fan of writing lists." I could hear him smoking and I was jealous I couldn't. "Pretty sure she wrote a list after I came out to her."

"I guess. Anyway, how was your day?"

"Jamie is afraid to sit next to me in class." He said.

"Well you were pretty direct."

"Somebody had to be. I don't like mind games."

It lit me up inside to hear him say those words. We said goodnight soon after as I still had my list to write and he had more reading to do.

"*Mijo*" My mother said when I got off of the phone. "I was only teasing when I said about Simon." She gave me hug. "*El tiene sus estudios* and you have to think about yours."

"I know Ma."

I gave her a kiss on the cheek and went to my room.

I put on a mix tape that Si had made for me not too long after we had met. I turned off all the lights apart from the one next to my bed. "My Funny Valentine" by Chet Baker was the first song that played. I laid down on the bed with a blank sheet on top of a copy of *Genre* magazine and thought about what it was that I liked? What could I study?

I woke up in the morning with the light still on and my back hurting from the awkward position I had fallen asleep on. I looked at the piece of paper which had some drool on it.

Si

Writing stories

Reading books

Reading people

My friends

History

The Village

Listening to music

Talking to people

Hazelnut Coffee

Watching movies

Diners

The Piers

Dancing

Photography

Fun

As I re-read the list, it became clear that I had more thinking to do. I folded the list and put it in my journal. I stretched my back out on the bed and looked up at the ceiling fan.

Seven

Uncle Jose's tombstone was a rose colored marble which I chose. His stood out amongst the row of somber black and grey ones; it was a fitting tribute to a man who stood out in life. I could feel him nearby, flapping his rainbow wings and making a comment about how Cuchi and my mother looked like grieving sisters competing for attention. I wasn't sure if it was planned but both were dressed in near identical dresses cut just above the knee and wearing their tiniest gold jewelry. Cuchi had a small veil on her wig that would have been disrespectful if anyone else had worn it.

Si and James were both dressed in dark suits, as were Guillermo and Hector. Arturo wore a blood red rose in his lapel and he held onto Hector. He looked the part of the mourning husband and I guess it was right he should. *The husbands that never were.*

The sun was shining and it was warmer than it had been for days. Even for an Indian summer. I had a feeling that was Uncle Jose's doing. He loved to wear shorts as long as possible throughout the year. Unlike my Mother who couldn't stand the heat, he missed the warmth of Puerto Rico. When he first got sick, he said as soon as he recovered, he would make his way somewhere warmer like Miami or Key West.

My mother and I knelt down and she reached out for Arturo to join us. He stood next to her and tears were falling from his cheeks. She held him tight and gave him a kiss. He put his right hand on her arm. I said the Lord's Prayer in Spanish out loud.

We put down a bouquet of roses we had bundled together at home with red, orange, yellow, purple and white roses. He loved color and the bouquet did not disappoint.

I looked at my mother who was holding back tears and put my arm around her. Arturo was beside himself. I looked up and Guillermo was nearby but with enough distance to respect the family moment. Uncle Jose would have liked him. I liked him. I half smiled at him and he bowed his head.

She got up, pulling Arturo and myself with her. She wiped her eyes with both hands.

"*Bueno.*" She said. "*Sabes que Jose no le gustaba esta pendejeria.*" She pointed to her tears. "Let's go dance and eat, *como le gustaba.*"

"*Así Así.*" Cuchi said and clapped.

We all hugged each other and when I got to Si, I felt like I could collapse into his arms. He held me up and kissed me on the cheek.

"That was beautiful."

"Thank you for being here."

"Always." He kissed me again.

"*¡Oye!* Cuchi said to us. "This is a cemetery not the Rambles."

Si and I both laughed. James stood there shaking his head at Cuchi.

"*¿Qué es eso?* My mother said to Arturo.

"*Mami,* you don't want to know."

We walked back to Hector's minivan and headed to his restaurant. He had his staff prepare a buffet for us. We sat around a large table in the center of the restaurant with the sound of trickling water fountains and some of Uncle Jose's favorite music playing through the speakers. No sad music, just happy dancing music like Willie Colon, Donna Summer, La Lupe, Madonna, Tito Puente and Celia Cruz.

The somber mood of the cemetery had given way to a *fiesta*, a celebration of Uncle Jose and everything he stood for. Outside the restaurant people went about on their normal Saturday shopping while we danced. It was the perfect memorial for him, it was the funeral he should have had but then life was very different then.

Hector danced with Arturo as old friends. They giggled and laughed as they reminisced about their younger years. I had never seen Hector so happy and he was the kind of guy who was always smiling. He danced with Cuchi who made him blush as she teased him with her seductive dancing. Mrs. Chan came out of the kitchen, took one look and went back in. I had a feeling she was less impressed. She didn't enjoy speaking with people and that day was no exception. My mother danced with both Arturo and Hector to "Oriente" and for a moment, I pictured them younger, as kids on a sun soaked island, far away from the concrete of New York. They were missing two though, Uncle Jose and my dad. They were there in spirit, dancing in the empty spaces.

"Shall we join them?" Si said and held his hand out to me.

"You're gonna dance to La Lupe?"

The music had changed as I got up. It was a favorite of Uncle Jose's "Get into the Groove."

"Saved by Madonna."

Si pulled me up and we joined everyone on the dance floor. We danced close and I forgot where we were or that my mother was there until I heard her voice.

"Eeeew." She said and laughed.

"Grow up Ma!" I said and continued dancing.

It was about late afternoon and Hector's staff was cleaning around us. My mother was a little tipsy along with Arturo. She raised her glass of wine and toasted to Hector's generosity.

Hector stood up and put his hand on his chest.

"*Familia. Todos.*" He pointed around the room. "All of us."

Guillermo ordered us a car service to take Si, James, Cuchi and myself downtown. Arturo decided to stay longer with my mother and Guillermo. It was like the adults sending the kids to bed but I didn't mind. He was afraid of anything happening to us because of how Cuchi was dressed.

"*La calle esta dura.*" He said.

It was a saying that my mother used as well about the streets being unsafe.

"*Ay* Guillermo." Cuchi said. "You don't know what I normally have to do to get a taxi." She put her arms around him and gave him a kiss on the cheek, leaving a lip mark that made him blush.

"Eh Eh" My mother said which made us all laugh. "*Ese es MI hombre.* That's MY Man."

Si had his arm around me. I looked at them all. They were my family and I couldn't have imagined my life without them.

The car Guillermo had called was driven by his friend Julio who Cuchi took an instant like to. She sat in the front seat and batted her false eyelashes from the moment the door closed. He played some Exposé and Cuchi was dancing the cabbage patch as best as she could with a seatbelt on.

"Damn *Mami*, you can move." He said and moved his shoulders along with the music.

"*Papi*, you don't even know the half of it." I wondered what Rafa would make of the scene but then I never asked what their relationship status was and I wasn't sure they knew or cared as long as they had fun.

"Expo-don't over there." James said to Si and Me. He shook his head at Cuchi in that judgmental next door neighbor way.

Si was moving his head to "Come Go With Me." I looked out the window as we headed towards Manhattan. I closed my eyes and felt Si grab my hand as I drifted off. The day had been emotionally tiring but I was glad we celebrated the anniversary with others. It could have been just Mom and me but with everyone there, it was special. Arturo being there made it perfect. To have my boyfriend and my friends there was something I hadn't even thought possible when Uncle Jose died.

The piers were coming into view and we turned up 10th Street. Julio's freestyle tape was now playing "One Way Love" by TKA. Cuchi and Julio were still moving in the front and James looked at them in disbelief.

"Gurl, I feel like somebody's about to cut a Valencia cake or something?" James said.

I laughed.

"What's that?" Si said.

"It's the bakery of choice for Latinos." I said and patted his knee. "Be thankful my mother lets me choose my own cakes now. Trust me."

Julio dropped me us off on the corner of Bleeker and Christopher.

"How much is that?" I asked.

"That's alright *Pa*." He said. "Guillermo took care of it."

He gave Cuchi his card before she opened the door.

"Anytime you need a ride *Mami*, you call me."

"*Papi*, I got a man already." She said and put the card into her bra.

"That's alright *Mami*. I ain't trying to take the place of your man. You know what I'm saying." He winked at her and she gave him a kiss on the cheek.

We all looked at her as he drove away. She adjusted her dress and then looked at us.

"What?"

"Gurl." Is all James said.

I grabbed Si's hand as we crossed the street in the direction of Fat Cats. It felt right to be back in The Village on the anniversary of Uncle Jose's death. It would have been where he chose to go on a Saturday night. Although things had probably changed since he last went out, there were still places where time may have stood still, like Julius', The Two Potato or Ty's.

We had agreed to meet Rafa and Michael at Fat Cats. When we got there, they were playing pool. Rafa had a cigarette hanging off the tip of his mouth as he leant over the table and took a shot. The juke box was playing Tina Turner's 'Better Be Good to Me." Cuchi lip synched along to it and danced towards him. Michael got Rafa's attention and he put his pool cue down and held his arms out for her.

James danced his way to Michael who looked embarrassed but couldn't look away. He shook his head and smiled.

"Thank you." I said to Si.

"*Te amo.*" He gave me a kiss on the lips.

"*Je t'aime.*" I said. It sounded weird coming out of my lips and I wasn't even sure I was saying it right. I just hoped he understood. Seeing Arturo at Uncle Jose's grave made me think about how important it was to take a chance in life. I didn't want to stand at a grave one day and wonder what could have been.

"*Très bien.* Practicing a bit of French?"

"You never know when I might need it." I said.

"Indeed." He wrapped his arms around me.

Michael called us around the pool table. "You guys up for something different tonight?"

"What you have in mind baby?" James said and put his hand on Michael's shoulder.

"There's a bar in the East Village called The Boiler Room. Want to go?"

Cuchi looked at Rafa who nodded his head to say he was up for it.

"I don't know girl, I may need to change first."

"Why?" Rafa said.

"Honey Xavy does alternative better than Cuchi."

"Hey" Rafa said and put his arms around her. "Cuchi can do anything."

"And she does." James said which made us all laugh.

"Alright fine."

Si and I looked at each other.

"Sure. But we need to change." I said.

We headed back to ours so we could freshen up and change. James borrowed a blue GAP t-shirt from me that fitted him better than it ever did me and some jeans from Si. I changed into some baggy blue jeans and a maroon long sleeve shirt like the skater boys in Washington Square Park wore. Si put on my favorite outfit of his, green cargos, red converse and a black t-shirt.

Rafa and Cuchi amused themselves with MTV which was playing "Smells Like Teen Spirit." They were banging their hands to the music. Michael looked at them confused.

"What?" Cuchi said. "Isn't this what the East Village boys listen to?"

"Umm. I think they listen to all sorts of stuff, like we do." Si said.

Cuchi and Rafa took a taxi but the rest of us decided to walk. The evening had chilled down from the warm spell we had earlier that day at the cemetery. Changing clothes made it feel like two separate days.

Although I was tired on the way downtown, I felt ready to take on the night. The walk from west to east was refreshing. Everyone we passed seemed like they shared one thing in common with us wherever they were headed, they were out to have a good time.

James grabbed my arm as we passed the arch in Washington Square Park. He held me back to let Si and Michael walk on ahead of us. They were in a deep discussion about music from what I heard as there was a mention of The Ramones and CBGB's.

"Thank you again for the other day."

He patted my arm. "A pleasure. You two talk then?"

"Yea. I think we're gonna be okay."

"You gotta try, right?"

"Yup." I said. "What about you and Wonder Bread?"

James laughed. "Girl, you remember everything, don't you? It's alright. No it's not alright. It's better than alright. It's nice."

"But?" I said in a low voice as I didn't want Michael and Si to hear what we were talking about.

"We're struggling to get a little time alone, you know what I mean?"

I gave him a confused look.

"Don't make me say it." He said.

Then it hit me.

"Ooooh." Of course with James living with his grandmother and Michael up in Westchester. Where would they get together?

James nodded his head.

"Leave it with me." I said and patted his arm. I was pretty sure Si wouldn't mind if they stayed at our apartment the weekend we were going to his parents. It felt so grown up to be going away together. It was the next stage of our relationship. I don't think we had spent an entire weekend just us since we got together. There was always BiGLYNY and friends to hang out with. I hadn't really thought about it till then.

When we got to the Astor Place Cube. Michael grabbed one of the tips and started to move the cube around. He had a childish smile on as he did it.

"I've always wanted to do that." He said to us.

It was like seeing the city through his eyes. I hadn't thought about the cube before. It was just there and most of the time, there were people hanging around it so I never took much notice of it. A kid about 10 years old was pointing at it and looking at his mother. Michael called the kid over and he helped him push it. The kid laughed as Michael helped him. I saw a look in James face as he watched the scene that made me think I had just witnessed him falling in love.

"C'mon baby." James said to him.

The kid's mother thanked Michael and the little kid shook his hand. Michael was smiling ear to ear and he walked over to James and gave him a kiss. Si grabbed my hand and we all walked on.

Cuchi and Rafa were smoking a cigarette outside The Boiler Room with a tall blonde guy who was by the door.

"Marco." She said. "These are my friends."

"Hey." We all said in unison which made him look at us a bit strange.

"You guys have ID right?" He winked.

We all nodded.

"Good." He smiled and opened the door for us. The bar was dark and smelled of stale vodka, cigarettes and weed. The juke box opposite the entrance was playing Depeche Mode's "Things You Said." I looked at Si and we both smiled.

Cuchi and Rafa were less impressed.

"Gurl, we gonna have to hit that jukebox and perk this shit up."

Rafa nodded his head in agreement.

Michael led the way to the bar and it was the first time I had seen him relaxed in a gay bar. We had been to Uncle Charlie's and Splash but because he was so handsome and fresh faced, all eyes turned to him whenever we walked into those bars and he was uncomfortable with that feeling of being fresh meat. It was the opposite for me. I enjoyed the attention because for so long, no one paid me any.

The bartender was waiting for us with a half grin when we got to the bar. There were a few people sat at the bar, a couple looked up at us to take notice but no one stared. It was a first for us as a group. I saw the bartender look over at Marco and then smile.

In the time I had come out, I had learned that the gay scene operated under its own set of rules. Bartenders and doormen turned a blind eye as long as you didn't cause too much of a scene or bring unnecessary attention to yourself. For us, there weren't that many places we could go especially as the weather turned cold, so we made sure not to get kicked out of the places we did get into.

"Oh my God. They have cider." Si said very loud. "Lu, you have to taste this stuff. It's really popular in the UK." His face lit up like the Christmas tree at Rockefeller Center. "Two ciders please."

The bartender acknowledged and poured our drinks. Michael and James ordered two beers.

"What do you two want?" Si said.

Cuchi and Rafa were by the jukebox choosing songs.

"Two red wines." Rafa said.

The bartender gave them an odd look but shrugged. He grabbed a dusty bottle of red wine that did not look like it had been touched for a while.

Depeche Mode faded into an upbeat track that I recognized instantly. We all looked up at one another as the music was familiar but the words were in Spanish. I turned towards the jukebox and Cuchi was lip synching to Tony Basil's "Mickey." Rafa's eyes were wide open as he clapped along. Cuchi did her best to imitate the music video without the cartwheels. The bartender had a smile that made him look younger than his shaved head did. He seemed to welcome Cuchi's energy. She continued to dance around the bar and made her way to wherever anyone was sat. The older guys in the bar laughed along but a couple of younger guys looked less impressed by Cuchi's performance.

One of the younger guys said to the bartender in a high pitch voice. "It's too much in here. We're going."

The bartender waved him off with indifference as the guys left in a huff.

"Okaaaay." Si said to the bartender.

The bartender leant over the bar and I could see that through his baggy shirt, he had a defined chest underneath. He smelled of sandalwood like the incense you burn when you're trying to cover up the smell of weed.

"You know what fags are like these days, they don't like anything too gay." He said in a Southern accent. He smiled and rolled his eyes toward the door.

Cuchi overheard the bartender.

"I hear you. Can take it up the ass but can't handle all this in their face." She rubbed her hands up and down her body and made a face like Marilyn Monroe being seductive.

"That's it honey." The bartender said. "So what's your name?"

"Miss Cuchi Fritta." She extended her hand. "Which I guess means nothing to a Southern white boy like you."

The bartender stood up and put his hand to his chest. "Honey, I've been with enough Puerto Rican's to know what a *cuchifrito* is." The word sounded so funny with a Southern drawl. Tommy as we later found out was from Athens, Georgia.

Cuchi clapped her hands together.

"Oh shit. We got a salsa queen here." She said and then pointed to Si. "Another one."

"Honey, men is men." Tommy said. "Life's too short to discriminate."

"Thank you." Si said and high fived Tommy.

I rolled my eyes and shook my head. Si could be such a dork at times but he was my dork and I loved that he made no apologies for being a dork. I looked over at Michael and James who were deep in conversation.

"*Dassit.*" Cuchi added.

James and Michael looked at me and smiled. It looked like James had told him about looking after our place while we were away. I asked Si for a moment alone.

"No domestics." Cuchi said as we excused ourselves and went to the far corner of the bar where there was a sofa.

"What's up?" Si said and put his arm behind me on the back of the sofa. He was sat as close as he could without being on top of me. It was nice to be that close. I didn't feel claustrophobic.

"You know we have that weekend planned, right?"

"Yea." He looked down at me in a suggestive way that turned me on.

"Well." I thumbed his shirt. "How about we let James and Michael stay at our place?" I said. "They're struggling to get time alone."

"Of course." He said and kissed me on the neck. "I remember those days trying to get time alone." He kissed me again. "In private."

The sensation from his lips on my neck made me giggle and I turned to him and kissed him. Our mouths both tasted of cider. In that dark corner, I wanted him so bad.

"Boys." Marco said. "Anymore of that and I'm going to have to start charging you by the hour." He smiled as he sat on a bar stool by the door.

We both laughed and got up from the sofa. After an adjustment, we headed back to the bar to join our friends. I caught James' eye and nodded. He mouthed a "thank you." Michael looked over and winked in that way I was getting used to from him.

The jukebox started playing "Only Love Can Break Your Heart" by Saint Etienne. I recognized it from one of mixed tapes that Si had gotten from his cousin in London. He put his arms around me from behind and danced against me, moving me along with his body. I could hear him singing along.

"Oh this is alright for white boy music." Cuchi said out loud to Si and smiled.

Si stuck his middle finger up at her and blew him a kiss.

She mimicked grabbing it and then smacked it against her ass.

"Who is this?" Rafa said.

"*Saint Etienne.*" Si responded.

"Who?"

"They're from England." I added and continued to move my body with Si. It felt like a continuation of what had started on the sofa. We were never that affectionate at Uncle Charlie's or Splash but there was something about being at The Boiler Room that made us feel free. It was like anything could happen.

"Oh okay." Rafa said.

Cuchi grabbed him and they danced together. For all her protests about heading East, she looked like she enjoyed herself, but then it was hard to think of a place that she wouldn't enjoy herself.

It was a very different way to spend a Saturday night and though we were all together, at times we were in our own pairs. The week of guidance counselors and chats I was unprepared for dissolved into the evening. Si and I couldn't keep our hands off each other and it reminded me of the summer where apart from going to work, the days were about having as much fun and hanging out as much as we could.

The bar was packed by the time we decided to leave. All of us were pretty buzzed from the alcohol and Cuchi had reached that stage where the heels needed to come off so in her words, "it was time to go." We tried to get her to change before heading home given the problems she was having with her parents but she waved us off as she stood outside the bar and smoked a cigarette.

"They're away visiting my *Titi* in Philly." She said. "Anyway, Ricky is working the door tonight and unless he wants Mr. Finkleberg in 501 to know he's been banging his daughter, he won't be saying shit."

"Does that mean there is room for me tonight?" Rafa asked.

"Always room for you." Cuchi said and kissed him on the lips.

"Can Michael and I stay?"

"Gurl, like you even need to ask." She winked at James and Michael.

"Thanks." Michael said. "Shall I get us a taxi?"

Cuchi nodded and blew him a kiss.

We decided to walk as the air was crisp and it was a nice relief from the sweatiness of the busy bar. It seemed like a waste of money to take a taxi to the West Village. We said our goodbyes and made our way up St Mark's Place. The street was busy and lit up with signs for tattoos, piercings, records and clothing. We stopped off at St. Mark's Pizza for a slice which helped soak up some of the cider.

We continued west heading down 8th Street. It still struck me how a wander down that very street only months ago would change my life forever. When we got to the top of Christopher Street and Greenwich, I took Si's hand in mine.

"Do you want to get some chocolate cake?" I said.

He put his arms around my waist and held me.

"That sounds like a plan."

We walked towards Caffe Raffiella through the side streets towards 7th Avenue South.

On our way into our apartment building, we ran into Roberta.

"Hey kids." She said as we held the door open.

"Hey Roberta?" I said.

She stopped and smiled.

"Do you remember at my birthday, you said that you had a story about my Uncle?"

She nodded.

"We went to his grave today and I'm curious, what was it?"

Roberta pointed outside with a nod of her head and we followed. She lit a cigarette and offered us one. She adjusted her long beige coat.

"Many years ago when I first came to the city, I used to work the piers." She said and took a drag. "You know, most of us girls did."

She exhaled. "One night, there was guy who let's just say was getting rough." She took another drag and exhaled. "I was trying to scream but this asshole had his hand on my mouth but I must've screamed loud enough that somebody heard me."

I could see in her face that she was reliving that moment but I didn't dare touch her or move.

"Anyway, next thing I know is that I'm free and this guy is being kicked down to the ground. I mean by the time he was on the floor, he was all bloody and could barely move." She smiled as she recounted that part. "This handsome man in a leather harness hands me my purse and asks me if I'm alright."

She wiped her eye.

"That man stayed with me till I calmed down and even came down to the piers the next few nights to make sure I was okay."

I looked at her. Si put his cigarette out and held me.

"Jose was a good man." She said. "Next time you go to the cemetery let me know, maybe I can go with you or you could put some flowers down for me."

"Sure." I said. "That would be nice." I hadn't expected a story like that and yet it was good to hear that he was so brave. That he had protected someone who I would be friends with later on.

She put her cigarette out and smiled in a maternal way.

"Good night kids." She said and walked away.

Eight

Si was on the sofa reading when I woke up. He was listening to Chet Baker on a low volume. I wiped the sleep from eyes and yawned as I wished him good morning. He put his book down, got up and gave me a kiss. I half hugged him in that still asleep phase of waking up.

"Coffee." I said.

"C'mon." He patted me on the back and I followed him into the kitchen.

He poured me a cup of coffee and leant against the kitchen counter with his arms folded. I took a sip of coffee and let the aroma wake me up.

"You studying?"

"Needs to be done." He said.

"Yea, I have some to do too."

"Study date it is."

He gave me a kiss on the forehead and went back into the living room. He put the volume up on the stereo. I drank that cup of coffee and poured myself another one. The sky was gray outside and it looked like it could rain. Fall had definitely set in. I walked back into the living room to sit down at the table when I heard my beeper go off.

Si looked at me and I looked at him. I went into the bedroom and grabbed my pager from my jeans on the floor.

"Mom." I said to Si and went to the phone and called her.

He returned to his book. "Give her my best." He said without looking up.

"*Bendición.*"

"*Dios de bendiga mijo.* How was your night?"

"It was good Ma. You?"

I could hear a noise in the background which sounded like her bed creaking.

"*Bueno mijo.* You know."

"You still in bed? Actually, don't answer that."

"*Ay Luis*, grow up. I'm a woman as well as your mother." That was not the conversation I wanted before a second cup of coffee.

"If you're coming home tonight, you'll have to make yourself dinner or eat before, ok?" She said.

"*¿Por que?*

"We're going to City Island for dinner."

"Oh." I said. "We is it? *Entonces me quedo aqui.*" I looked over at Si and I saw him smiling. He was picking up more Spanish with each day we were together.

"Okay *mijo.* I love you both. Do your homework."

"I'm about to. *Te veo mañana.*"

I put the phone down and Si looked up at me. He had a silly grin on his face.

"Another night together?"

I nodded my head. "Want to go and get some breakfast?"

"Sounds good." He put his book down and we both got dressed.

There was plenty of time to shower later as we had the whole day and night.

Si wanted the challah French Toast from Manatus but they had a 40 minute wait so we ended up at Tiffany's which was busy but we were able to get our usual booth by the window. We stopped off at Espresso Bar on the way back to the apartment for some large hazelnut coffees and chocolate croissants or *pain au chocolat* as Si insisted on calling them. He put on a Dinah Washington compilation while we both worked on our assignments at the table. It was nice but distracting sitting across from him. I couldn't help playing footsies with him.

"Finish your homework then we can play." Si said.

"Promise."

He looked up at me and grinned before returning to his book. My beeper went off but I didn't recognize the number. I showed it to Si who had no idea who it could be. I called the number.

"Lu?" It was Michael.

"Hey, is everything ok? Where are you?" I said.

"Nothing." He said. "I'll make this quick as I'm at Grand Central. If Mel asks, I stayed at yours, okay?"

"Why? What's up?"

"It's all cool, just that I told my parents I was at Mel's and they checked up so I had to tell them I stayed with another friend." He sounded tired. "I have to run. Can we walk later this week?"

"Sure. Speak soon."

I put the phone down and Si looked up at me.

"All good?"

"Yea, Michael needed an alibi for the night."

"Ahh."

Si and I were lucky that we didn't have to keep those secrets from our parents but we were also aware of how rare that was. For most of our friends, a white lie could mean the difference between having a home or not. We kept them and carried them out of safety and protection. It was the hypocrisy forced on us by the world. We're told not to lie but sometimes lying becomes the only way to survive.

I shook my head trying to get the thought out of my head. I looked over at Si and felt that feeling in my stomach that he gave me by just being in my life.

"Hey Si."

"Uh-huh." He said and looked up at me.

"Will you come with me to the college fair next week?"

"Of course." He blew me a kiss. "Get back to work."

Nine

Melanie *fucking* Sputano was in a mood when I ran into her outside the7-Eleven. It looked like she had been waiting for me to get off the bus.

"Was Michael with you or James?" She said his name in a sarcastic voice.

"Hi to you too."

"Sorry. Hi. So?"

"Yes he was with James but he stayed at mine."

"Oh." She looked at me to see if I was lying. "What does he even see in him?"

I threw her a filthy look.

"James is smart, funny, a great person and he's attractive. What's not to see in him?"

"You sure you don't like him?"

"I have an amazing boyfriend already, thank you very much."

"Yea, He's pretty fly." Mel said. "I just worry about Michael that's all."

I put my arm around her and we walked towards the school.

"I know. He's got us though. We look out for each other."

I wanted to be back downtown with Si and not at school that day. If he hadn't had to work that afternoon, I would have stayed with him and played hooky but he was right to make sure I made it school. We had a good situation. With my mother dating Guillermo, we could see each other as much as we wanted and I also didn't worry about her. There was a trust. Still, my mind was on the sofa with Si's arms around me.

When we got to the school, Mel's friends were waiting for her and one of them rolled their eyes when she saw us together. I made a *fuck you* face at her. We said goodbye and I walked on. My beeper went off as I walked into the building. I recognized the number from the one that Michael called me on. I went downstairs to the pay phones. I passed Joey who winked at me. He was hanging out near the cafeteria doors like he was waiting for someone. I gave him a strange look and called Michael who let me know that his parents believed him so all was good and that he wanted to meet after school.

I put the phone down and walked out of the cafeteria. I bumped into Joey who was still there. He was biting his nails.

"Oh, sorry." I walked on.

"It's okay. I already have it." He said.

I stopped and turned around.

"What the fuck did you say?" I clenched my fists and blood rushed to my face.

He took a step back and put his hands up in the air.

"It was a joke, Luis. Calm the fuck down."

"Joke? Have what? What the fuck is wrong with you, you freak?"

He laughed which made me nervous. Was he alone? Were there others waiting for me?

"Freak? Thanks." He started to walk backwards and then stopped. "I thought you out of all people would know how it feels to be called that."

He stared at me and when I looked into his eyes, it hit me like a swinging door to the face.

"Wait? You're?"

He smiled like a kid who had let out a surprise he was dying to share or he would explode. The bell rang for homeroom but we remained the only ones in the basement hallway. I realized as I looked at him that he hadn't been teasing me about being gay but just didn't know how to approach me. It was strange but that didn't matter. I felt like a dick for calling him a freak.

"Joey." I took a step towards him. "Why didn't you just tell me?"

He shrugged his shoulders. "I'm not as cool as you." He looked away for a moment and then back at me. "Why would YOU want to hang out with me?"

"Me?" I said and put my hand to my chest as I was about to clutch my imaginary pearls. "I'm many things but cool is not one of them."

"Oh please, don't give me that shit." He said. "Last day of school you just came in and didn't care what anyone thought, you screamed you were gay and pretty much told the rest of us to deal with it." He laughed. "I could never be that cool. I know I'm strange. Always have been."

I walked up to him and put my hand on his shoulder. "I'm sorry for calling you a freak." It was wrong of me and I knew why I did it. If I judged them first, then it took away their power. Joey wasn't one of *them*, though. He was one of us.

He smiled. "Thanks."

"You want to go grab some breakfast? Talk a bit more?"

"Yea." He said. "Yea. I'd like that."

We headed out the side entrance near the football field down to the diner on the square. The only person who I knew that would look for me was Mel and I was sure she was in class. We sat at a booth towards the back. Joey sat with his back to the rest of the diner. The waitress brought us menus and we both ordered coffee.

"You boys eating?"

"I'll have the pancakes." Joey said.

"French toast for me please."

"Oh a polite one." She said and sneered at Joey.

Sitting across for him, I saw him for the first time. He wasn't a bad looking guy. He dressed like most of the guys at school in rolled up Cavaricci's and those shirts with one too many buttons undone. His hair had too much gel and was slicked back to a point that it made his face look angry but he had a sweet smile and light brown eyes that made up for his fashion choices.

He waited till the waitress was out of hearing distance and leaned in towards me. "So when did you know?"

"I think I always knew but it wasn't till last June that I really knew, if you know what I mean."

He smiled. "Is that when you met your boyfriend?"

"Yea." I said. "And my best friends."

The waitress came back with our coffees and slammed Joey's in front of him. She winked at me. Joey paid no mind to her passive aggression and put four sugars in his coffee.

"He's a lucky guy." He said without looking up at me. His Italian-American Bronx accent made him sound like a parody of a mobster.

"I think I'm the lucky one." I put one sugar in my coffee and stirred it.

He stirred his coffee and looked at me very serious. "Don't talk yourself down. HE'S the lucky one."

He made me think of what Cuchi said the night of the Columbia dance. Was I enjoying the attention? Was that what it was with Scott too? Joey wasn't queeny like the rest of us and maybe that's why I thought he was strange. He was awkward and wasn't sure how to act. I remember when I first came out not knowing what was the right or wrong way to act until I realized there wasn't one.

My head was spinning with thoughts. I needed to move the conversation along. "So, what about you?"

He looked around again. "You remember that show *ChiPs?*"

I nodded.

"Well I used to watch it cos of Ponch but I didn't know why cause no one in my family ever talked gay stuff or nothing. I don't even have gay cousins. We're Italians, you know."

I tried not to roll my eyes. "Okay."

"Last year though when you came in that 2QT2BSTR8 t-shirt and you had them rainbows and pink triangles on your back pack, you walked in like you owned the place. I knew then that I felt the same way about you as I did about Ponch."

"Um. Wow." I said. "Do you know how freaking scared I was

even though I knew Anthony probably wouldn't attack me?"

"Yea. Why didn't he? I mean his face went crazy when he saw you but he just walked away." Joey had an intrigued expression on his face.

The waitress brought our food to the table and Joey made it a point to thank her loudly. I was sure I heard her call him an asshole under her breath.

"So?" He continued. "What did happen with Anthony?"

"Let's just say a friend talked to him." I smiled.

"What? Like some kind of gay mafia?" He said and laughed.

"You can say we're a family." I tried to imitate a sort of mobster face and accent but I probably looked and sounded more like a mob wife. "I was looking ahead that day because I was scared to meet anybody's eyes, not because I was confident."

"Well." He shrugged and poured syrup on his pancakes. "You fooled me. I just remember thinking wow, that's who I am. That's what I like."

"I'm flattered Joey but…"

He put his hand up. "I know you've got a boyfriend and I'm no home wrecker. If anything changes though." He picked up his coffee cup. "Call me." He winked and then took a sip of his coffee.

I didn't know which way to look. *Did that just happen?* Also, why did I think it was sweet as well as creepy? What was this thing about being cool? Luis Morales was never cool? I wasn't even sure Lu was cool. I considered myself lucky more than cool.

. I took a sip of coffee. "I'll keep that in mind." I said and put syrup on my French toast. *Thanks* felt like a lame response and as odd as the moment had become, it was nice to know that I wasn't the only gay boy at school. "Do you ever go downtown?" I asked.

"Nah, hardly ever leave the neighborhood, you know."

"Do you want to hang out in the Village sometime?"

He looked at me a little surprised. "Isn't that though really gay?"

"Aren't you?" I said.

He laughed. "That's good." He pointed at me with his fork.

I invited him to BiGLYNY anytime he was ready. I figured it would be good for him to meet other people and hopefully move on from his crush on me. We finished our breakfast and headed back to school in time for second period. Joey went his way and I went mine when we got to the entrance.

After school, I saw him as I walked to the bus stop. It was the first time he didn't say anything out loud to me. He smiled and put his head down like he was shy. I could see a grin on his face.

I waited for Michael outside the McDonald's with my headphones on. Liz Phair was singing "Johnny Sunshine" and I moved my head along to the guitar sound, very much in my own world. I felt a tap on my shoulder and turned around to see Michael. He had a stoner smile and his eyes were squinty. I took my headphones off.

"Hey."

He motioned with his head to follow him. "Looking good Lu." He giggled. He then patted my shoulder and put his arm around me, held me tight before releasing me. "Good to see you."

I side-eyed him. "You okay?"

"A little high." He said. "Smoked half a joint on the way here. Want some?" He smiled ahead at nothing in particular.

"Sure." I said, given how stoned Michael was it would have felt too much like I was missing the joke if I hadn't and the day had been strange enough with Joey. "What happened this weekend?"

We crossed Fordham Road and headed in the direction of the university and the Botanical Gardens. Michael pulled out the half smoked joint and lit it before passing it to me.

"My mom found a flyer for Limelight in my room." He lit a cigarette. "They started asking questions." He took a drag and exhaled. "It's cool though, I got them off my back."

I took another hit of the joint and passed it back to him. I could already feel it and it was time to stop if I was going to face my mother later. "Do they know?"

He shook his head. "No, I denied it all. I just need to make it through the next year and its college. Then I won't have to worry about them." He laughed. "Anyway, I think they would be more upset about James than him being a guy if you know what I mean."

I snorted. "Yea. Mel said."

He continued smoking his cigarette.

"I wanted to see you." Michael said. "The weekend was fun and it's hard to get to the city during the week. I mean I talk to James every day but it's nice to have someone to talk to face to face." He smiled at me.

"I get it." I replied. It was easy for me to head downtown. For

Michael and Joey, things were different. We now formed a secret club that existed in plain sight just by being friends. We shared something others around us didn't and I remembered how much I wish I had had that before I came out. I told Michael about Joey coming out and our breakfast conversation.

Michael laughed as he put his cigarette out. "Why does it surprise you that he feels that way?" he said and stopped in front of me so he could look at me. We were stood opposite the main entrance to the Botanical Gardens.

I looked away and then up at him. He was smiling down at me. "I don't know. I spent my life either being picked on or being ignored. Kinda hard to think of anyone thinking I'm cool or cute."

"Lu." He put both hands on my shoulders. "You're hot inside and out. I say that as a friend but also as a man." He looked at me as if he was scanning me for a response.

I laughed. It was the only response I had. He put one arm around me but it wasn't a romantic gesture.

"C'mon." He said and we walked onto Fordham University campus.

The campus was like another world compared to what surrounded it. The grass was a lush green. There were large trees that shaded the buildings and dorms. You couldn't hear Fordham Road or any traffic. It was like a bit of country in the city, almost like Central Park but there you could still see the tall buildings that surrounded the park. We headed towards the McGinley building which was the student union building because Michael needed to use the phone. I sat outside the building and watched students. I felt out of place even though I wasn't dressed any different than they were. It was more that I knew that I was from the other side of the tracks. Given that the Metro North tracks separated the campus from my side of Fordham Road, it was accurate. I literally was from the other side of the tracks.

What a day? I thought to myself. First there was Joey, then classes and then Michael. It felt like I had lived three different days in one. Everyone at school kept talking about the colleges they were thinking of applying to and all I was thinking about was a weekend away with Si. That was another aspect of going away to college that I didn't want to think about, leaving my friends. I had only just made friends. What if I didn't make any new ones? Would I go back to being that lonely kid again?

"You'll grow old quick."

"Huh." I turned and Michael was back from his call. "Grow old quick?"

"You looked lost in thought." He said and sat next to me. "My grandfather used to say to me as a kid, not to think too much or you'll grow old quick."

"Ahhh. Okay."

"James says hi."

The mention of James made me smile. "You guys looking forward to spending the weekend together?"

Michael looked up. His eyes were more visible and he was chilled. "We are. It'll be nice to experience a bit of what you and Si have." He bumped into me in a playful manner. "Be together without worrying about when and where."

"I'm glad." I said. "You guys speak a lot during the week?"

"Every day."

James never mentioned that they spoke so much but then why would he? I didn't tell my friends everything Si and I did. I liked that there were things that were just between us. They were safe from jokes, from bitchiness, from shade. Those little things were like a warm blanket you could carry anywhere with you and wrap yourself up from the cold.

Michael put his hands in his pockets. "So you think this weekend you'll go away?"

"Most likely." I said and looked ahead. "I have to ask my mom but pretty sure that's just a formality. Is it that different being in the country from being downtown?"

He pulled a card out of his pocket and handed it to me. "This is my direct line at home. Let me know later."

I took the card and tried not to laugh. Of course he had a direct line and of course he had a calling card. Why wouldn't he? My beeper went off and it was my mother.

"Shall we walk?" I tapped Michael with my shoulder.

"Sure." He said. "But just to clear the air. I hope you know what I said earlier was true but not in a weird way."

I got up and extended my hand to him. "Of course and you're hot yourself." I said. "Even Si thinks so."

He laughed, took my hand and got up on his feet.

"I think I'm falling in love with James."

I felt a rush of warmth inside as I heard those words.

"You should tell him." I said.

"Maybe this weekend I will." He said and grinned like he had the moment planned out. "I know Mel can be a bit much but I'm glad she introduced us."

"Me too." I said to him as we approached the Metro North Station. He gave me a hug at the entrance to his platform. "Speak soon."

"Look forward to it." He then disappeared down the stairs and I walked up Fordham Road.

When I got home my mother was singing along in the kitchen to "Brujeria" by El Gran Combo, it was playing on the radio. She hadn't heard me come in and I watched from the entrance to the kitchen as she danced in that way that you do when you're sure that nobody else was watching. She turned from the kitchen sink towards the table and caught sight of me.

She held her hand out to me and I danced towards her. I twirled her around the kitchen and moved along to the brass sounds. We laughed and sang along together. I couldn't remember the last time we had been silly like that and it was liberating. As a child, I would step on her feet and she would guide me that way as we danced. I wasn't a child anymore but I was still her kid.

The song faded out and a commercial for Tops in the Bronx came on so she lowered the radio. We looked at each other and laughed.

"How was school? *Mijo.*"

"It was weird but okay."

"*¿Como?* She sat down at the table.

I sat down with her and told her about Joey but didn't mention his name as I didn't think it was my place to. I also didn't tell her about him having feelings for me as I didn't want to think about it anymore than I had.

"*Pero mijo*, another friend is good, no?"

"Ma, just because we're both gay doesn't mean we're gonna be automatic friends." I said.

She raised her hands up. "Okay okay, *calmate.*"

"Can I go away this weekend with Si to his parents house Upstate?"

"*Mijo*, we were supposed to go see your *Abuela.*"

"Maaa." I whined. "Can't we do that another weekend?"

She gave me a serious look then cracked a half smile. "Fine *pero abuela, proxima* weekend, ok?"

I walked over and gave her a hug. "Thank you Ma. I love you."

I couldn't wait to tell Si.

Ten

Jackie was the happiest I had seen her in a while. In fact, the last time she was that happy was when she threw out some Upper East Side princess and her mother who tried to tell Jackie how to take her daughter's photo "properly." She not only forcibly threw them out but set the $5000 check on fire in front of them. It was my first week on the job.

She had just returned from Sag Harbor that morning and she was glowing. It turned out she ran into an ex girlfriend from her college days.

"It was amazing Lu." She said "After Steph, I thought, that's it Jackie. Fuck women but don't get involved again, life will be much happier that way."

She wasn't smoking or drinking red wine. I had never seen her not do one of those things in the time I worked for her. It turned out the ex, Lisa was "just going through a phase" when they dated in college and had broken it off to go out with the guy she would end up marrying.

"Total Wall Street prick. Too much coke not enough balls." Jackie said and laughed. "Thank God they never had kids. Total deal breaker for me."

It was scary and unnatural to see her happy but also kind of nice in an unnerving way.

"Are you around this weekend?" She asked me.

"No. Sorry. Going Upstate with Si."

"Alright. Can you reschedule the Feldman shoot? I need you with me for it and as you have plans."

"You sure?" I was freaked out by that point. What alternate universe had I walked into?

She walked up to me and put her hands on my shoulders. "Lu, you have to grab love and hold onto it." She tapped my shoulders. "Don't fuck it up. Don't let 20 years pass by."

"Um okay." I walked over to the phone and left Jackie standing with her thoughts. She looked as if the world had fallen into place.

After work, I headed up to Oscar Wilde to surprise Si. I pushed the door open and saw him at the counter. He was pricing a box of Audrey Lorde books. He looked up as the door closed behind me.

"Hey baby." He said in a soft voice that made my stomach go funny in a good way.

I walked over to the counter and kissed him on the lips.

"Can we hang out tonight?"

"Every night." He said and walked around the counter. He wrapped his arms around me and I took in his smell. He hadn't worn the Fahrenheit in a while and it was comforting. It reminded me of the first night we spent together. The week had been long and I was already exhausted. There was no one else I wanted to be exhausted with but Si.

He had a bit more time before he could close up so I helped him finish pricing books as we listened to Pet Shop Boys *Discography*. It felt much later and colder when we closed the shop. November was knocking on the door and it wasn't even Halloween yet.

We walked down towards Sheridan Square holding hands.

"You hungry?" Si asked.

"Yea."

Tiffany's looked busy from across the street and I wasn't in the mood to run into anyone else. I thought Manatus would probably be the same. There was Fudruckers but I wasn't sure I wanted a burger.

"Let's grab a pizza pie." Si said.

I looked at Si. "You always know the right thing to say."

"C'mon."

We walked down Barrow Street towards Bleeker Street Pizza. I waited outside while Si ordered. The place was packed with unfamiliar faces. It seemed like we weren't the only ones who didn't want to cook that night. Si liked to call Tuesdays "Gay Sunday." It was the one night of the week that there was less going on for us than other nights. It was a night for laundry, chilling out and watching TV. I was ready to give into "Gay Sunday."

We took turns carrying the warm white box back home. The smell of the sauce and cheese was intoxicating and there were greasy spots forming on the pizza box which made our stomachs growl.

Roberta was standing by her door when we walked past. Si offered her a slice which surprised her, at least judging by her look it did. She took a slice out of the box and grinned.

"This don't mean you can stop by and borrow a cup of sugar though."

"Wouldn't dream of it Roberta." Si said.

We continued up to our apartment. We barely made it to the kitchen as we were both hungry and desperate for a slice. The oil from my slice was dripping onto my hand but I didn't care. Pizza to me was a gift from Heaven above and I could live off it given the choice.

"Mmmm. So good." Si said.

"Mmmm." There were no other words, just enjoyment.

After we finished a few slices, we changed into our pajama bottoms. There was enough pizza left for breakfast and that made me smile.

Si sat down on the sofa and I collapsed into his arms. I laid my head on his chest and he put his arm around me.

"What's up Lu?"

I dug my head into his chest. "Been a weird start to the week."

"Anything you want to talk about?" He asked. His voice was soft and inviting. I wanted to tell him then about Joey, even about Michael but more than anything, I didn't want the moment to change. I didn't want things to get awkward and all that other stuff didn't seem to matter too much at that time.

"Just school stuff mainly." I said and looked up at him. "Can we leave it for tonight?"

He kissed me. "Let's leave it all outside tonight."

"How about you?"

"Been tired I guess." He squeezed me with his arm. "Happy you're here though." He looked into my eyes. "Very happy."

"Me too."

I reached over to the coffee table, picked up the TV remote and handed it to him. He turned on HBO and *The Goonies* had just started. The opening credits were rolling as The Fratelli's drove their SUV in the race on the beach as part of their getaway plan.

"I love this film." He said in a loud high pitch voice that made me laugh. He smiled like he had just been given the best surprise. I leaned further into his arms and the week began to drift away as the film started.

There was no better way to spend a Tuesday night than on the sofa with my boyfriend watching *The Goonies*. I could handle the world and anything that it threw at me as long as it was the two of us together.

It was still dark outside when I woke up. Si was still asleep, his bangs covered his face and looking at him made me horny. Spending the night together was just what I needed. I was looking forward to the weekend more and more by the second.

I wrapped myself in my bathrobe and went into the kitchen. There was enough coffee for about half a pot and I wrote "buy more coffee" on the magnetic notepad on the fridge before heading back to bed while the machine made coffee.

Si had turned around when I returned to bed. I slipped under the comforter and pressed against him. He made an *mmmm* sound. He pushed his bangs back and I could see his eyes were half opened. He made a sniffing noise and grinned.

"Coffee and this." He said as he turned to face me. "Be careful or I'll get used to this."

I looked into his eyes and smiled as if I had no idea what he was talking about. "Get used to what?"

He rolled on top of me and gently kissed my lips. I knew then I would miss homeroom that morning.

I got off the train at Westchester Square and though I had some leftover pizza with Si before we both went our separate ways, the morning fun had left me hungry still. I headed to the diner to order a ham, egg and cheese sandwich and a coffee. I sat in one of the booths near the entrance. I was in my own little word, lost in the memory of the morning when Joey walked in. He was dressed in those colorful baggy pants that the guys in my high school liked to wear. He had on a black bomber jacket with the fur trim around the hood.

"Hey." He said. "Thought I'd find you here." He sat down and then called out to the waitress. "Can I get a coffee over here?"

"Not until you say please." She said with a disgusted look on her face.

"Sorry honey. Can I get a coffee please, thank you."

"That's better."

I shook my head. I think Joey thought of himself as a gay version of Andrew Dice Clay but he came across more like Joe Pesci in *Goodfellas*.

"Hey Joey." I said.

"So I was thinking about your offer and yea, I guess it wouldn't hurt to meet other guys." He slapped my arm which took me by surprise. "Might even get lucky, right." He laughed in a way that made him sound more creepy than cool.

Unless he toned it down, the only thing he was going to get was read and I already pictured Cuchi's face as she did it.

"Cool. How about next weekend?"

"Why not this weekend?"

The waitress came back and put his coffee down and rolled her eyes at him. She then came back with my sandwich and coffee.

"Sorry about the wait doll." She winked at me.

"Not a problem. Thank you."

She patted Joey on the arm. "See! Manners! They don't cost nothing."

I took a bite of my sandwich. The egg yolk broke which covered the ham, cheese and bread into one gooey mess. It was my favorite way to eat the sandwich. I then put it down and wiped my hands with a napkin. I was the first to admit that it wasn't the sexiest food to eat.

Joey asked me again about the weekend.

"Going away with Si."

"Oh." He looked away and then back at me. "The boyfriend." I wasn't sure if he was teasing or trying to be funny but his tone sounded bitter and after the morning I had had with Si, I wasn't in the mood to deal with his awkwardness.

"Yea. But if you wanted to go this weekend, I could introduce you to some of my friends and you could meet up with them."

"Nah." He made a gesture with his both his hands. He looked disappointed. "Nah, don't worry. Some other time. Anyway, I'd rather go with you." He tried to smile but it didn't work. "Off anywhere nice?"

"Upstate. His parents have a house up there."

Joey's eyes opened wide. "Wow. So his parents know about you two AND he's some sort of fancy rich guy."

I never liked to think about Si as some rich boy. It was unfair and he was never a snob or judgmental about anyone no matter how little or how much money they had. The label just wasn't him.

"My mom knows too so I guess we're both lucky."

"Yea you are." He smiled and it was genuine.

He sat and drank his coffee while I finished my sandwich. We walked up to the school entrance together. The bell had just rung and there were students going in and out of doors. You could hear the steps on the stairs and the rumbling noise of idle voices.

"Thank you Luis. For listening and stuff."

"It's cool. Friends?" I said and held my hand out to him. "My friends call me Lu."

He shook my hand and then pulled me towards him and gave me one of those straight boy hugs.

"Friends, Lu."

He went to the left of the entrance and I walked to the right. I turned to see him but he didn't look back at me and I was happy about that. I had another friend at school.

Eleven

I met up with James and Cuchi at Tiffany's after work so I could pass on my set of keys for the weekend. Si was up at his parents for the night, so it was just the three of us. I couldn't remember the last time; it was just the three of us. I told them the whole Joey story.

"Oh gurl, one of *them*." Cuchi said.

"What do you mean?" I asked.

"You know." James said. "One of them I like dick but I'm not gay like you cause you dance to Madonna and shit and I don't."

They both snapped their fingers at the same time. I missed their double act.

"Michael doesn't dance to Madonna." I said.

James looked at me and looked as if he was about to say something bitchy but settled on "true."

"Rafa doesn't either." Cuchi said. "You think it's a Bronx thing?"

"I dance to Madonna."

Cuchi looked at James and then they both looked at me.

"Well" Cuchi started to say.

"Oh fuck you!" I blew a kiss at her. "Bitch!"

I was still learning not to walk into traps like that but it was all harmless fun and no matter how much we teased one another, we were solid. Like a pack, we had each other's backs.

"Anyway!" I said. "You know what the whole macho thing is like when you're Italian or Puerto Rican."

They both nodded their heads.

"Just be nice when you meet him. Plus, I gotta see my *abuela* that morning so you know…"

Cuchi put her hand on mine. I noticed a chip on one of her press on nails. "Alright *Papi*. Promise."

"Thanks *Mami*." I put hand on top of hers. "How are things at home?"

Billy walked by and picked up the menus without saying a word. We all had coffee and water as I had promised to have dinner with my mother later that night. She was making lasagna or her Puerto Rican version of lasagna which meant lots of *adobo* and *sazón*.

Cuchi threw her hands up. "Gurl." She looked at both of us. "You're not gonna believe this." She took a sip of water and cleared her throat. "You know my bitch sister Laura, Miss Never Does Anything Wrong."

James and I nodded.

"Well, she was the one that first got my mother all worked up about me dressing up. The *pendeja* then figured out that we all stayed at the house when they were away and she told my mother." Cuchi stopped for a moment. Took another sip of water. "My mother was all crossing herself like she was appealing to *Dios* himself and my father just stood there with this look of death on his face. Gurl, I thought he was going to kill me."

"What?" James said.

"You know you can always stay at mine." I added.

Cuchi raised her hand to stop us.

"Listen to this right." She said. "My father makes us all sit down and pulls out a pregnancy test that he found in the bathroom and looks at Miss Lady of Our Immaculate Conception." She took a deep breath for dramatic effect. "The bitch starts crying and wailing."

"Noooooo" I said. "Damn."

James had his hand on his chest and was shaking his head in disbelief.

"I know riiiiight?" Cuchi said. "Turns out Miss Thing was trying to deflect from herself by getting me in trouble."

"So what happened?" James asked. "Don't keep us waiting."

"I'm trying bitch!" Cuchi snapped. "Right, so then my mother starts again with her *Dios Mio*, what did I do God? My father though was like Concha, stop with the Martyr shit, it's tiring and he looks at Laura and is like I'm not mad at you. Whatever you decide, we'll be here for you." She took another sip of water. "Then he turns to me and says Xavy, it doesn't matter to me if you dress up or not. It never has." Cuchi put her hand on her chest. "Gurl, I nearly cried and he put his hand up to all of us and said, what bothers me is the lies. *Se acaban hoy*. No more lies in this house."

"Wow." James said.

Cuchi nodded. She looked free for the first time since the dressing up scandal began. She could be herself and spread her fabulous wings again. I reached over and put my hand on hers and squeezed.

"Thanks *Papi*."

"So does that mean we will see more of Cuchi and less of Xavy?" James asked.

"It means you'll be seeing more of me in whatever motherfucking form I feel like bitches." She laughed and clapped her hands loud. She looked at us both and reached out for our hands. "I love you. Thank you for putting up with my shit."

"Please." James said and smiled.

I could only smile back. I was so happy to see Cuchi shine again.

Billy came by with the coffee pot. "Let me guess." He said.

Cuchi got up and put her arm around him. "Baby, I got a man now but remember always what we could've had." She then gave him a kiss on the cheek and left a lipstick mark.

Billy looked at her expressionless. His cheeks were flushed and we all laughed.

When I got home, I was thinking about my friends as The B52's "The Deadbeat Club" played through my headphones. It was the perfect soundtrack to the night we had just had. My mother was sat in the kitchen with Guillermo. He had stopped by to drop something off or so he said. I didn't want to ask any further on that subject. He still seemed a little nervous when I would come home to find him there. He acted like he wasn't sure if I was okay with his presence.

"Luis." He got up and shook my hand. "I was just about to leave."

"*Siéntate* Guillermo." I said. "Have dinner with us. You're always welcome."

I could see in my mother's eyes that she had been waiting for that moment. The moment that *the man of the house* gave her the final approval. I had always thought of her as *the man of the house* but I guess like with everything else, I was entering a new chapter in my life and although I wasn't sure what to expect or how I would handle it, I was ready for it.

Twelve

When I returned from the bakery on the Grand Concourse with a loaf of warm buttered bread, my mother had coffee ready and on the table. She was sat in her blue nightgown with matching robe. My hands were warm from carrying the bread but I could feel the morning cold on my cheeks and nose.

She pulled the steaming bread out of the paper bag and broke the loaf into smaller pieces. She put them on a large plate on the table for both of us to eat.

"Is Simon picking you up *acqui?*" She asked.

"Huh." I said. Though I had gone outside, I felt half asleep and I had forgotten to ask him the night before. I looked at the clock on the kitchen wall. It was 6am. "I'll call him after we eat."

"Okay *mijo.*"

"What are your plans this weekend?" I took a sip of coffee and although I loved the coffee that Si and I drank when it was just us, I couldn't deny that a sip of Café Bustelo was like a bucket of water thrown in your face to wake you up.

"Guillermo wants to go to *el cine.* Watch a movie." She sighed.

"Since when do you like going to the movies?" I asked. She could never sit still long enough to watch a film in the theater. I don't think it was *just* timing that she lived to see VCR players become the norm in her lifetime.

She smiled. "*Mijo,* I'm more than just your mother, ok."

"Too early Ma." I shook my head.

"Ahh I see. You can have a life *pero yo no.*" She threw a small piece of bread at me.

The phone rang and we both looked at each other like *Who could that be?* I got up and answered it.

"Hey baby." It was Si.

My mother rolled her eyes like she was mocking me and continued to eat with a grin on her face.

If we couldn't wake up together, hearing his voice on the phone first thing was the second best way to start the day. Although I still had to get through the day, my mind was already on the weekend ahead. I was in my own little world when I put the phone down. I turned around and my mother was making kissing noises at me.

"Oh Ma, grow up." I said and returned to the table.

"*Mijo*, you're happy. I'm happy. *La Vida es Buena.*"

She was right about that. "He's picking me up at 4."

"I'll make sure I'm back from work but if not, *llamame* ok?"

She got up from her side of the table, walked over to me and gave me one of her maternal kisses on my forehead.

"I will Ma."

I let her use the bathroom first to get ready while I finished my coffee and bread. Afterwards, I went into my bedroom and pressed play on the cassette player. Pat Benatar's "Shadows of the Night" was halfway through. I looked at my unmade bed and the clothes on the floor. I didn't know where to begin. I emptied one of my backpacks and thought about what to pack. *What did I really need for two nights away?* I came to the conclusion that the whole point was to spend time together. I sang along to Pat as I threw some underwear, socks, a couple of shirts, some condoms and lube in my bag.

I stayed on the Pat Benatar kick that morning and was bopping my head to "Love is a Battlefield" when Melanie *fucking* Sputano caught up with me as I walked towards the school entrance. I shut my music off and said hello.

"Is Michael with you this weekend or James?"

"You know most people start conversations with a hello." I said.

"Sorry. Hey Lu. So?"

I sighed. "He and James are staying at our place while we're in the country." It sounded so grown up when I heard it out loud. I couldn't help smile.

"Why does he have to lie to me?"

I shrugged.

"Maybe he doesn't want to get you in trouble?" I said. Though what I really wanted to say was that it was none of her business but it was too early to be confrontational.

"Oh." She stopped and thought about it. Just as I had figured, she had made it about her. "I love Michael, I'd always protect him."

"Maybe you should be having this talk with him and not me."

She looked like a light bulb had just gone off over her head. "Yea. You're right." She then linked her arm around mine. "So the big weekend huh. It should be beautiful up there with all the leaves and stuff."

I looked at the trees as we walked past them. They were starting to change color but there was something dirty about them. Maybe it was the pollution from the expressway or just the city. I was excited about seeing what the trees and nature looked like Upstate. I imagined the colors would be brighter and bolder. Maybe it was like one big unfenced botanical garden.

"I hope so."

As we approached the corner, I saw Joey and he waved hello at me. Mel looked at him and then me. "So you two?"

"We're friends. I have a boyfriend as you know."

"Hey, gay or straight, guys are guys and in my experience when a guy likes you, he'll keep letting you know."

"I've made it clear that we're just friends and wait, how did you know?"

"I'm not blind Lu." She said. "I see the way he looks at you and don't worry, I haven't told anyone."

I hadn't thought about Melanie *fucking* Sputano having gaydar or maybe Joey was just that obvious. She unlinked her arm from me and gave me a kiss on the cheek.

"Have fun this weekend." She then crossed the street and met up with her other friends. I continued walking to the main entrance of the school.

Thirteen

When I got home, I finished packing as I listened to a mix tape that I hadn't played in a long time. I was trying to match the vocals of Ann Wilson on Heart's "Alone" as I put in some pj's, a pair of jeans, a sweater and *Everybody Loves You* by Ethan Mordden in my backpack. A boyfriend who worked in a bookshop was a bonus. Thanks to his discount, my bookshelf of gay writers went from nonexistent to pride of place in my bedroom. The last thing I packed was a 35mm film case which had some weed I got from Cuchi and a pack of E-Z Widers.

I laid on my bed after packing my bag looking up at the ceiling fan as I always did when I let my mind wander. Heart had given way to the rockier sounds of The Bangles and then The Go Go's "Worlds Away" was playing when the intercom buzzed.

I knew it was Si when I pressed the voice button.

"Be right down!"

I turned my stereo off and took one look around my room. Something in how it looked to me had changed. I turned the lights off and rushed down the stairs. Si was standing outside his parent's Jeep waiting. He looked so out of place in his khakis, converse and black turtleneck that I let out giggle. I wanted so bad to hug and kiss him hello but I also knew what our neighbors were like. He opened the trunk of the car and put my bag in it.

"You ready baby?"

I smiled. "Oh yea."

He shut the trunk and we were about to get into the Jeep when I heard my mother's voice.

"*Mijos un momento.*" Her voice traveled and it seemed like everyone in the block had turned around at the same time.

She gave us both big hugs and kisses. "*Cuidanse.* Call me when you get there."

"Okay Ma." I gave her a kiss and noticed of one our neighbors, *Doña* Cessa looking at us with disapproval. She was one of the God fearing hypocrites that my mother couldn't stand.

My mother followed my eyes and turned towards *Doña Cessa's* window. "*¡Oye! No miras aqui que su hijo esta en Rikers,* ok?" The hypocrites never liked being reminded of their delinquent sons.

Si laughed which surprised us both. *Doña Cessa* slammed her window shut. My mother blew us both kisses and we got in. Si turned on the engine and we waved goodbye as we headed towards the Major Deegan Expressway with Julian Cope's "World Shut Your Mouth" playing.

"I made a new mix tape for the drive." Si said.

I put my hand on his knee.

We had crossed into Yonkers when I noticed that the traffic was heavier going into the city. I turned around and looked at the lights we were heading away from. By that time, we would be in the Village, getting ready for whatever night was ahead of us. It was an odd but nice feeling to be going the opposite way.

Si was moving his head and singing along to Violent Femme's

"Prove My Love." He glanced at me and blew me a kiss.

"You okay?" He asked as he looked ahead at the road.

"Yea, well sort of."

He overtook the car ahead. "What's up?"

I lowered the music a notch. "Remember I told you about Joey?"

He smiled. "Weirdo at school."

I giggled. "Yea."

Si continued to overtake cars. "Let me guess. He's in love with you."

I couldn't tell if he was teasing or being serious.

"Well I don't know about love but he's definitely attracted to me. How did you know?"

Si smiled and let out a little laugh. "You're gorgeous that's how I know." He said without taking his eyes off the road. "I see how other guys look at you."

I looked at him and then ahead. "Does that bother you?"

He shrugged his shoulders. "Sometimes. Does it bother you when a guy finds me attractive?"

"Sometimes." I didn't like to admit that but I also felt that in the silence and confines of the car, the space was safe and I could admit things that needed to be said. "I worry more than anything. That you'll find someone more like you and that I'll be just this fun thing you had and that's it."

Si got into a position on the road he was comfortable with after overtaking about 5 or 6 cars. He put his hand on my knee and pressed it for a moment.

"You are more than just fun for me." He said. "I knew the moment I laid eyes on you through the bookshop window that I wanted to meet you."

"Wait. What? You saw me standing outside?"

He glanced at me and I could see he was smiling. "Of course. I was afraid you would get cold feet or something. You looked so lost and nervous and beautiful."

"Wow." I knew the moment I saw him that I wanted to meet him. To talk to him. I never thought he wanted it first.

"Why are you surprised?"

"I kept thinking why he would want me when he could have anyone. That's why I'm surprised."

"Thing is Lu, so could you." He said and I could see his expression turn serious. "You're not the only one who worries, you know."

I had never thought about things like that. Even though my life was better than it was a year ago, the truth is, I still saw myself as a nobody. It was like I still had something to prove. I didn't feel comfortable if someone told me they liked me. But I also knew that the attention was nice and distracting.

"You can't help if someone finds you attractive" Si said. "Do you find him attractive?"

I shook my head. "No, he kinda creeps me out." That was true. Joey did creep me out but I also thought that part of the reason was that he was just coming out; everything was still all over the place for him so he reflected that.

"You know, there's no law that says you have to be friends with every gay person you meet." He then paused. "It could also be that he has a coming out crush on you."

"Coming out crush?"

"Yea, you know, you're the first gay person he meets and he feels safe so he has a crush on that."

"Huh. Maybe." I liked that. It made sense.

"If he creeps you out though, don't be friends with him."

"That simple?"

He laughed and pinched my knee. "It's that simple baby."

"I love you."

"I love you too baby and you're stuck with me." He said.

I sunk into the passenger chair and let his words envelop me. I couldn't imagine a world where we weren't together. "I'm happy with that."

Alice Cooper's "Poison" came on and I put the volume up. We sang along as we drove towards the Tapan Zee Bridge. The house was just outside Cornwall on Hudson, which Mr. Trelawney chose because he was from Cornwall and found it funny.

It was pitch black when we turned off Route 9 to get to the house. The house was set back from the road and surrounded by tall trees. A motion light came on when Si parked the car outside the garage. Compared to their brownstone on the Upper West Side, the house was simple. It had two stories and a covered porch that wrapped around the house. The silence was almost deafening. The stars were clear and bright. I had never seen them shine like that before. I took a deep breath and then coughed as if something had gone down the wrong tube.

"Your lungs are clearing." Si said. "C'mon."

We stepped onto the porch and it creaked just like it would in a film. There was swing sofa that hung from the porch roof. I could see us sitting on it together under a blanket with cups of hot chocolate. Si opened the screen door which screeched and then unlocked the front door. He turned the hall light on and the first thing I saw was a staircase opposite the door. There was a narrow hall to the left of the staircase that went towards the back of the house and on either side of the entrance hall were two rooms.

"Wow. This is beautiful." I said.

He put his arm around me and kissed me on the cheek. "Let me show you around."

The house had a library/ lounge, a living room, a dining room off the kitchen to the back and a small family room with a TV. Behind the house were a swimming pool and a hot tub.

"You kept that a secret." I said. "I didn't bring a bathing suit."

"I wanted to surprise you." He switched on the pool light and a beautiful oval blue shape lit up the night. There was a hot tub just at the far corner of the pool. "Oh and you won't need a bathing suit."

We went outside and he walked over to a box near the pool and flipped a switch.

"For later." He said.

The air was cold and crisp. I could see my breath and I imagined the pool would look like a witch's cauldron when it heated up and the steam met the chilly air.

"C'mon." He grabbed my hand and guided me back to the house. He was like a kid showing off a brand new toy and a carefree smile that made me melt.

Upstairs were two bedrooms, one bathroom and the Master bedroom with its own bathroom. It was the only room that was made up.

"Guess this is where we're sleeping?" I asked.

"It's the biggest bed in the house." He said and put his arms around me. He pushed me against the bed and landed on top of me.

I looked deep into his brown eyes and lifted my head to kiss him. He pushed his mouth onto me and our tongues met. I lifted his turtleneck up and felt the little patch of hair on his chest that I liked to run my fingers through. He sat up and took the turtleneck off and then lifted my shirt off me. He got off the bed, stood up and unzipped his jeans. They fell to the floor, he wasn't wearing any underwear. My eyes lit up as I looked at him. He stepped out of his jeans and bent over to take mine off. In one move, he took off my jeans and boxers. He pulled me up by the hand and kissed me as we stood there naked, our bodies close together.

"C'mon."

I followed him downstairs and outside. The cold air hit my body as we ran towards the hot tub. Si climbed in first and pressed the button that turned the bubbles on. He held his hand out for me to grab as I got into the bubbling water. I had never been in a hot tub before so I wasn't sure what to expect. My upper body was exposed to the chilly October air and my lower half was nice and warm in the comfort of the water. It was a feeling I could get used to and reminded me of when you slept with one foot from out under the covers to keep your body temperature balanced.

Si moved closer to me and sat with his back against my chest. I wrapped my arms around him and I looked up at the sky. The stars were so clear, even with the pool light on.

He sank into my arms and my chin just about touched his ear.

"Mmmmm, Lu. I've been dreaming of this all week."

"Thank you." I said.

"You're welcome." He pointed up at the sky. "That's the Big Dipper over there."

I had only seen it in textbooks but it was easy to make out. There was the ladle and the handle. "That's so cool."

"That's about all my knowledge of the stars." He giggled.

"More than me. I've never seen them so clear outside of a planetarium."

"Not even in Puerto Rico."

"I was about two years old the last time I went to PR."

He put his hand up to mine as I held him. "I'd love to show you where my dad grew up in Cornwall." I held him tighter as he looked up and smiled. "The stars are amazing."

"When was the last time you were there?"

"Last year. We used to go back every year but now every two years. Mum doesn't like the journey. She can just about handle the flight to Paris and the drive up here these days."

"Is it far?"

He smiled and lifted my hand out of the water and kissed it. "It feels about as far as you can get from the world. From London we used to either rent a car at Heathrow and drive or take the sleeper train from Paddington.

"Like the bear?"

"Exactly."

Months ago, my world was small. It was The Bronx mainly and *Abuela's* in Bayonne. Places like London and Paris were names in books or on TV shows. Cornwall was a place I didn't know existed. Even The Village was just a place I heard about when I stayed up and eavesdropped on Uncle Jose and mom's chats. My world was getting bigger with Si and yet I wanted it to always feel safe, like it did when it was just the two of us.

"Do you think we'll ever go there together?" I asked as I held him tight.

"I want to go everywhere with you." He tilted his head up and smiled at me. I bent and kissed his lips.

I leant back and thought about the word *everywhere*. It was better than forever. It sounded better than forever. Forever was something people wrote on Hallmark cards or on their Trapper Keeper. No one wrote: *Everywhere*. I pictured what it would look like.

"Lu and Si, Everywhere." I said.

"I like the sound of that." He responded. "Let that be *our* thing."

We laid there soaking in the hot tub, enjoying the feel of wet warm skin on wet warm skin. I had a momentary thought about the gang and about our apartment but I pushed it out of my head. The weekend was about us.

"You hungry?" Si asked.

I hadn't thought about food at all but the mention of it made my stomach growl. We hadn't brought any towels down to the hot tub so we ran back to the house.

There was a small dresser in the family room just near the patio door with spare towels and we dried off there so we didn't drip water all over the floor. The house was nice and warm compared to outside. We wrapped our towels around our waist and went into the kitchen. Si went to the fridge and I sat at the breakfast bar.

"What's for dinner then?"

I could only see his hand tapping against the double door fridge as he looked in. "Hmmmm." I heard him say. "Ahhh, thank you dad…oh and thank you mum. Hello!" He let the door close as he pulled out a glass container and a bottle of white wine.

I leant over the bar to get a better view of what he was doing after he put the wine and container down on the counter. He was looking in one of the cupboards under the counter and pulled out some potatoes, garlic, onions and peppers. He stood up and was moving his hips in what I had I thought of as "Si's dance." He did this dance when he was at peace with things, or things were falling into place.

"You going to keep me in suspense?"

He turned towards me and said. "Let's call it, Si's one pan surprise."

"Which is?"

He grabbed two glasses of wine and brought them over towards the bar with the bottle. He kissed me. "Now it wouldn't be a surprise would it?" He opened the bottle of Louis Jadot Mâcon Villages and poured some into the glasses.

"To Everywhere." He looked into my eyes and clinked my glass.

"To Everywhere." I repeated.

"Right, you sit there." He pressed play on the little stereo system in the corner of the kitchen and the familiar voice of Chet Baker came on. It was one of his dad's favorites which I was sure is where he got it from.

He poured some water into a pan to boil the potatoes as he sang along to "But Not For Me." He looked over at me and sang out loud to me in a bad attempt at Chet's voice as he preheated the oven.

Si prepared dinner like he was performing a show to one audience member. Even though he was popular and everyone loved him because he had this way of making them feel comfortable, it was when I saw him in his element that I felt like it was the real Si. He was goofy and silly which made him hotter than he already was.

He put the partially boiled potatoes in an oven pan with cut up peppers, onions, garlic and buttered chicken breasts seasoned with herbs, salt and pepper. He poured some olive oil on top of all it and mixed it up before putting the pan in the oven.

After he closed the oven, he danced over towards me singing along to Chet. He grabbed my hand and pulled me up from the stool and put his arm around my waist. He held one of my hands up to his and we swayed together to the music. Dancing on a Friday night was nothing new for us but instead of being drenched in sweat under flashing lights, this was more like a gay version of an F Scott Fitzgerald novel. I pictured us in tuxedos dancing somewhere fancy with a big band playing and long legged cigarette girls going from table to table.

"How come we don't dance like this at home?" I asked him.

He looked at me and smiled. "I don't know. Why *don't* we dance like this at home?"

"We should."

"Then let's." He said those words like it was decided. He let go of me as the song finished and grabbed his wine, then handed me mine.

The CD then played "Time After Time." He clinked his glass against mine and like Chet sang, I too felt like I was falling in love all over again. I put my glass down and wrapped my arms around him. I could feel the wine making me float.

Si's one pan surprise was delicious. The chicken was tender, the roasted vegetables had a bite to them and the potatoes were crispy on the outside. We ate at the dining table by candlelight, still in our towels wrapped around our waists. I had chosen a Billie Holiday compilation to put on in the background.

"So why don't you cook like this at home?"

He shrugged and picked up a piece of chicken with his fork. "Guess it's easier to just go out or grab pizza."

I nodded. "Yea we do like our pizza." I took a bite of a potato. "This is so good."

"Thanks baby." He took a sip of wine. His eyes sparkled in the candlelight and I thought about how much I had picked up just watching Jackie at work because I wanted to capture him just like that on film. I took a mental picture instead.

"I want to do more of this. Just you and me."

He raised his glass at me. "You always know what to say to make me smile."

"I could say the same."

When we finished dinner, I loaded everything into the dishwasher which was a luxury that we did not have and phoned my mother as I had forgotten to do it when we arrived but in all honesty, it was the furthest thing from my mind when we were in the Jacuzzi. She didn't pick up so I left a message with the number to call me back in the morning.

Si was sat on the sofa with his feet on the coffee table flipping through the TV guide. "Anymore wine baby?" He asked.

I looked in the fridge and there was another French wine I couldn't pronounce. "Yea, a San-cer I think?"

"*Sancerre*" He said in perfect French. "Bring it in please."

I brought the bottle and corkscrew in for him.

"Here's the Sawn-cerr." I teased.

"You can correct my Spanish anytime." He said and stuck his tongue out at me. He opened the bottle and poured some into the glasses.

I turned off the lights and sat next to him on the sofa. He grabbed a blanket from the side of the sofa and laid it across us. We sank back into the sofa together and I put my head on his shoulder as he looked at what films were on.

"Ooooh. *Halloween* is on in about 10 minutes."

I sat up and looked around the room. "Are you kidding me? You want to watch a scary movie out here in the middle of nowhere?"

Si had a mischievous look on his face. "C'mon baby, I'll protect you."

"Famous last words in a horror film." I loved scary movies but being out in the country and watching them with no lights on felt creepy.

He put his arm around me and pulled me towards him. "I'll make popcorn."

"Jiffy Pop?"

"Only the best for you." He said and got up.

"Now you're talking."

I followed him into the kitchen and he got the Jiffy Pop from the cupboard. He took some butter out and put it in a dish to melt in the microwave. He did his little dance as he held the Jiffy Pop over the burner flame. The kitchen filled with small pops at first before a steady stream of pops expanded the foil on top. Once the popping had stopped, Si poured the popcorn into a large blue glass bowl, poured the butter over it and sprinkled salt on top. He shook the bowl so the salt could cover as much of the popcorn as possible.

We sat down as the film started. I linked one arm around Si's for protection. He grabbed a handful of popcorn and brought some of it to my mouth. I ate a few and he ate the rest.

I hadn't seen *Halloween* in years and re-watching it that night, it was scarier than I had remembered. It could have been the surroundings though. I jumped and grabbed his arm throughout the film which made him laugh. The popcorn barely lasted the first 20 minutes of the film and although a maniac could have busted into that house that night, I took some comfort in that fact that at least we were together.

Fourteen

It was so nice to wake up in an actual bed under such a big comforter. Our futon was comfortable but you could hardly sink into it. I turned over and wrapped my arms around Si's exposed shoulders. I noticed he had a few whiskers coming through on his chin and I brushed my finger along them, which made him stir.

"Hey…mmmm." He pushed my hand away and smiled in a playful way.

"You need to shave." I said.

He turned towards me and looked at my face. He touched my cheek with his hand. "And you have yet to start."

"Har har." I kissed him on the lips.

"Sleep well?"

I nodded.

"Told you I'd protect you."

"You did." I responded. Although you could hear birds on our street. In the countryside, it sounded like birds were using bull horns or something. Their chirps were amplified. I couldn't imagine a better way to wake up. The room was cold and that made being underneath the covers feel perfectly balanced.

"THIS is Heaven." Si said and just as he kissed me, the phone rang. He rolled over and picked it up.

"Oh hello Mrs. Morales. Just one sec."

He looked over at me and handed me the phone. He got up and

walked towards the bathroom turning enough to smile and tease as he knew I couldn't react to the sight of his beautiful naked body.

"Um, hi Ma."

"*Mijo ¿Todo bien?*"

"*Sí Ma, tienen una piscina y* hot tub."

"Wow. *Tengo que hablar* with his parents."

"Ewwww Ma."

"*Ay Mijo.* Grow up."

Si returned from the bathroom and lay on his stomach next to me. I ran my hand down to the small of his back which felt rebellious as I was on the phone with my mom. He blew me a kiss and then turned on his side and started to touch my chest which made me jump. I looked down at him and smiled.

"Gotta go Ma, love you."

I put the phone down without even hearing her response and rolled on top of Si. We kissed and held each other tight as we became one that morning. Our hands and tongues explored one another making it hard for us to keep the noise down. As we were in the middle of nowhere with no neighbors for miles, there were sounds that we made for the first time together and I couldn't believe the energy we had without having had coffee.

We lay drenched in sweat and smiles afterwards before Si suggested we go for a swim. When we got outside, the cold hit me instantly and any excitement I had down there retreated as we ran towards the swimming pool. Si dove in like an expert swimmer. I chose to cannonball and it was like sinking into the warmest bath I had ever been. When I came up for air, Si was floating on his back near me. I swam and grabbed his foot and he splashed around pushing water towards me with his hand.

The sky was blue and clear. I couldn't believe we were swimming naked in October. Si swam behind me and put his arms around me. The steam rose above the pool which added to the warmth. He pulled me in the direction of the Jacuzzi. We climbed over the barrier into the Jacuzzi and sat opposite one another. Si leaned his head back and sank into the water. His foot brushed against my balls as he stretched it towards me. He then moved towards me and knelt in front of me. He put his arms just above my waist which was under water and brought his face close to mine.

"So what should we do today?"

I pulled him closer to me. "Oh I don't know. Go with the flow."

He kissed me, stood up and revealed himself. I got up and grabbed his hand and we ran back to the house. We made it as far as the family room. There was no doubt that the countryside had its benefits.

We lay on the floor of the family room on top of our towels from the night before. I ran my hand around his nipple as he gently rubbed my back. My stomach growled. I looked at the patio doors and the clouds had started to come in. It looked as if rain was on the way for the rest of the day which didn't bother me at all. We didn't need good weather to enjoy ourselves judging how the morning went.

"Hungry." He said.

"Yea."

We got up and wrapped ourselves in our towels. Si went to the fridge and looked inside, then closed it and looked at me like he had come up with some master plan.

"Let's just snack and see what's on the movie channels today?"

"I brought some pot."

He smiled like I had said the magic word. "You get the pot, I'll grab the snacks."

I went upstairs and got the pot, rolling papers and our pj's' from the bedroom. When I returned downstairs, the coffee table in the family room was full of various containers filled with stuffed peppers with cheese, olives, sun dried tomatoes and little mozzarella balls. There was a bowl of tortilla chips, fresh salsa as well as Chi Chi's.

He went to sit down and then got up and grabbed a bottle of Evian water before plopping himself on the sofa. I passed him the papers and pot as he was a better roller than I was. I looked through the TV guide.

"*Sixteen Candles* is on." I said out loud.

"We have a winner."

The rain gave way to thunder that afternoon but it didn't matter as we got stoned, devoured the munchie food and we watched *The Addams* Family after *Sixteen Candles*. At some point we passed out on the sofa because I got up to use the bathroom and it was already dark outside. I could hear the rain and wind outside.

When I returned from the bathroom, Si was up and clearing up the containers. I was starving so when he suggested making dinner, I answered him with a kiss and a hug. Si got some steaks out from the fridge to sit on the side as he prepared the roast vegetables and sautéed potatoes. We listened to Depeche Mode as he cooked. "Everything Counts" was playing when he turned to me and said, "We definitely need to do more of this at home."

I loved the thought of doing more things like that with him. Just us. I knew that when we got back there was school, family, work, and friends but we could make time just the two of us, right? *Isn't that what you're supposed to do when you're happy in love?*

"Deal." I responded and walked over to where he was. I put my arms around him from behind and rested my chin against his back. I could still smell the both of us from that morning.

"Do you think your mom will let you stay Sunday night?"

"I don't see why not."

"Cool." He said. "Can you set the table?"

"Sure."

I lit the candles and opened the bottle of Malbec that Si had chosen for dinner after setting the table. The food smelled like it had been made in an expensive restaurant. Si was more of a cook than he ever let on and I was already getting used to it.

He poured the wine and raised his glass. "Everywhere." He winked and took a sip without breaking eye contact. "It gets harder to spend nights away from you." He picked up the pepper mill and cracked some pepper over his steak.

"I know." I took a sip of wine. There was something in his tone that made me feel like he had something to tell me.

He took a deep breath. "I finished my application for Paris. I haven't sent it yet though." He put his head down and cut some steak. "That's why I was at my parent's the other night."

I had a feeling that his mind was set on Paris but hearing it didn't make it easier and what did that have to do with spending nights away or together.

"That's great." I pushed the words out of my mouth and tried to put on a supportive comforting boyfriend smile. As much as I tried, my gut was doing somersaults and the beautiful meal he had prepared was the last thing I wanted to eat.

"Have you thought about colleges yet?"

"Not really." That was a lie, the more I didn't want to think about it, the more it lingered in my head. It was like a curfew I didn't want to obey. I kept my eyes on my plate.

I heard him put his utensils down.

"Lu?"

I raised my head slowly and met his eyes. The sadness in his eyes seemed to match what I was feeling inside. "I'm sorry. I know we talked about it."

He got up and crossed over to my side. He put his arms around me from behind and held me tight. "Baby, shhh. Don't apologize."

He was right. There was no reason to apologize. Neither of us should be sorry. I was angry. That's what it was. I was angry that I couldn't think about college without getting sad and that Paris was going to take away my happiness. I couldn't speak. Si kissed my neck which sent a shiver up and down my body.

He pulled my chair out a bit and knelt down in front of me. He took my hand and looked up at me.

"If you haven't made a decision about college, would you consider." He said and took a deep breath. "Maybe staying in the city and study…Maybe live with me?"

I gripped his hand tight and held it against my chest. I pulled it up to my chest and kissed the knuckles as I nodded. I stood up and pulled him up towards me.

"Yes." I said.

He held me tight and I felt his weight collapse onto me. I thought that he might want to break up because he would be away but he wanted to take it to the next level.

"Why don't we take a hot bath together after dinner?" He asked.

"That sounds nice." I said. I sat back down and though my appetite had disappeared earlier. I was hungry again after clearing the air.

The city had loads of colleges and my mother would love it if I was still in the city. I looked over at Si who looked as if the weight of the world had been lifted by asking me to consider moving in. That weekend was the first time I realized that I wasn't the only insecure one in our relationship. That I wasn't the only dork.

After dinner, I cleared up as Si prepared the bathroom. I went up to find him naked in the bathroom waiting for me. There were rain scented candles burning as well as tall white candles and the bath was a greenish color from bath salts. Si had Enigma's first album playing on a low volume. He came towards me as I entered the bathroom and kissed me before undressing me. He got into the bathtub first and sat up with his back against the back of the bathtub. I got in next and sat between his legs with my back against his chest.

He put his hand in mine. "You know my parents were married in Paris."

"You think we'll ever be allowed to get married?" I asked.

He kissed the back of my neck. "I do Lu. I do."

I closed my eyes and thought about whether he was right and if not, why could Si make me believe anything was possible? It had been that way since we had first met.

Fifteen

The fresh country air made my lungs feel clear as we walked in the woods holding hands. The conversation about Paris and college had lifted the tension between us and even though I was still no closer to choosing a college, at least I had a direction or at least an option. Apart from the birds and squirrels, it felt like we were the only living things on the planet.

"Are you going to miss me?"

"Like crazy." He kissed my hand and though it was a stupid question, I wanted to hear his answer.

We went for a final swim when we got back to the house just before the rain returned. Si got our bags together while I called my mother and told her I was staying in the city that night. We packed our stuff into the Jeep, and turned off the pool and secured the property. We stood on the porch as the rain pattered down, taking in our surroundings. The rain smelled fresh and clean.

"Can we come up here more?"

"I'd love that."

We ran to the car and got in trying not to get too wet. Si put his hand on my knee and I put my hand over his.

"Everywhere."

"Everywhere baby." He turned the ignition and it was like the moment had been staged when Pat Benatar's "We Belong" started playing on the radio. We both smiled as if Pat was in on our inside joke.

We stopped for gas on the other side of the Tapan Zee and I called our apartment to let the gang know we were on our way back.

"Hey *Papi*." I could hear Xavy washing dishes. I tried not think about what mess they could have made while we were away.

"We'll be home in just about an hour or so."

"Guys, the orgy needs to finish within the hour, okay." Cuchi had made a momentary appearance.

"Ewww. I hope not."

"See you soon *Papi*.

When I got back into the car, I told Si and we both looked at one another unsure if that was a joke or not.

Si decided he would take the car back to his parents the following day, so we parked it a few blocks from the apartment. The city felt dry like it hadn't seen any rain at all. I looked up at the building as we approached it and saw James and Michael on the fire escape. They waved when they saw us.

Roberta opened her door as we walked past like she had been waiting for us. She had her finger pointed at us and it reminded me of the mean old lady in *Gremlins*.

"Next time you leave the children alone, could you muzzle them?"

"Sorry Roberta." Si said. "Won't happen again."

She stared at us up and down. "I certainly hope not. I need my beauty sleep." She pointed to her face and body. "This doesn't come as easy as it once did."

I held in a laugh but I could sense that she knew I had. She closed the door and didn't break eye contact as if it were a warning.

When we got into the apartment, Rafa and Xavy were on the sofa smoking a joint. James and Michael came in from the fire escape. We all hugged and kissed and it did kind of feel like we had left our kids alone for the weekend. Si took the joint from Xavy, took a hit and passed it to me and then went around the group.

I put our bags in the bedroom and was happy to see the sheets had been changed and the bed had been made. We hadn't eaten since lunch so I suggested we all go to Tiffany's.

Rafa and Xavy put their coats on without hesitation. "Ready bitches!"

Si and I walked behind the group holding hands. Although the city wasn't quiet like Upstate had been, the space between us was just as peaceful.

Michael looked back at us. "The country did you two some good I see."

"And the city you two." Si said and pointed to Michael's hand in the back pocket of James' black jeans.

Rafa and Xavy were ahead of all of us and singing loud that 4 Non Blondes song that was everywhere.

"Gurl, I thought we were against animal cruelty." Si said very loud.

"Oh I see you're back from your shade sabbatical." Xavy responded.

"Missed me?"

"Welcome back, you shady bitch."

We all laughed and Si stopped walking and stepped in front of me. He looked down at me in that way that made me melt the first time he kissed me in front of The Center. He pressed his lips against mine and closed my eyes in the moment.

I heard a car drive by and some Jersey accent yell "Fags!" But it didn't stop us kissing. The car didn't even stop. I felt safe in that moment.

The incident didn't change our mood, if anything, Si held my hand tighter and we walked more defiantly. Michael and Rafa were new to The Village and they were angry.

Irena sat us in our usual booth. "My boys." She said in her Polish Brooklyn accent. "Coffees?"

We all nodded our heads.

"If that motherfucker would have stopped…I'd show him who's a fucking fag." Rafa said. His accent had gone full Bronx and there was a crazy look in his eyes.

"You and me both." Michael added.

James and Xavy looked at each other as if they were saying *we got some butch queens here.* Si put his arms around me and asked if I was okay. Thing is, I was. On a different day, my heart would be racing and I would hate the world for what it did to us but in that moment with Si, with my friends, the world didn't matter. The next time would probably be different.

"Guys, they were just assholes." Si said. "They didn't even stop."

"Exactly Si." Cuchi said. "Who are the real fags?"

"Why does fag have to mean weak?" Michael asked.

Irena returned with our coffees.

"It doesn't baby." James said. "Just what THEY think…Thank you Irena."

"My boys hungry? Yes?"

We placed our orders and Irena gathered up the menus.

Rafa was still angry. "Next motherfucker that calls me a fag though."

Xavy turned to him. "You know I'm the first one to open my mouth. Shut up James; don't make that face but Si's right. That bridge and tunnel piece of shit was too scared to even stop. Why let him ruin our time? Out there we have to deal with this shit but down here, this is our space. Don't let them take that from us. Don't let THEM win."

"Did you just paraphrase *The Goonies?*" I said.

Xavy looked at me. "It was on the other night."

"I know." Si said. "We were watching it too."

The Goonies lightened the mood at the table and I saw Rafa's shoulders loosen. He had his arm around Xavy and I think what made him angry was the thought that something could happen to him or to Cuchi and he couldn't protect them. We had all been called worse names than fag. The fact was, we were all protective of each other.

After dinner, being called fags was a distant memory and we left the diner having laughed with one another, at one another. The weekend was a reminder that we could have both the relationship and our friendships.

Si and I headed back to our apartment and smoked cigarettes in our boxers as we listened to The Sugarcubes with *MTV* muted in the background.

"I wasn't afraid tonight." I said to Si.

"No?"

"I'm not afraid when we're together."

He leaned in and kissed me. "Everywhere, baby."

It was the perfect ending to the weekend.

Sixteen

I was at the dining table finishing up some homework and drinking coffee when Si woke up. I got up early so I could make sure it was done before I had to leave for school. He walked over to me, kissed me on the head and yawned before he went and got himself a coffee.

It was still dark outside and it felt like a continuation of the night before. Si sat opposite me and picked up his copy of Rolande Barthes' *A Lover's Discourse*. He opened it and half smiled at me before looking down at the pages. It was such a peaceful way to start the day and I thought about how this could be our life in a years' time if I stayed in the city and we lived together full time. I could see it. We were basically living it already and I loved it. *Why wouldn't I want it to be like this always?*

 After I finished my homework, I toasted some bagels for breakfast and it was getting brighter outside. Si put on that Julian Cope song he liked to get ready to and I showered. Leaving the house that day felt different, our relationship had a direction. We were more than just together.

We walked together towards NYU so I could hop on the 6 train at Astor Place. On the corner of 8th Street and Fifth Avenue, Si kissed me.

"Speak later baby."

I waited for a second as he walked towards Washington Mews. He turned around and blew me a kiss.

I put my headphones on and pressed play on my CD player. Natalie Merchant's voice filled me with a sense of warmth as she sang "These Are Days." She sang those words for me in that very moment. Images of the weekend, Tiffany's the night before, the summer, the piers, new friends, all of it flashed in my mind. I smiled as I thought about how happy we were. How happy my mother was.

I didn't dread the ride Uptown to school that day as I usually did. When the subway left the tunnels after Whitlock Avenue, I put my sunglasses on as the sun was shining bright. The subway rolled on high above the Bronx River and although I couldn't see the downtown skyline fully, I knew it was there and it didn't seem as far away as it did a year ago. It lived inside of me. I was a part of it and it a part of me, like Si and I.

ABOUT THE AUTHOR

John Lugo-Trebble was born and raised in The Bronx. He now lives in Cornwall with his husband David and their three cats.

He is the author of *Lu's Outing* which is the first book in *The Everywhere Series*. His work has appeared in *Jonathan: A Queer Fiction Journal*, *Litro Magazine* and others.

You can find out more about him and his work at www.johnlugotrebble.com